"Le...
Melina aske...

John followed her across the room, vividly aware of the bed looming on his left. Melina stood in front of the window, silhouetted against the city lights and the night outside. The woman had a body made for sin. He stepped close behind her and looked over her shoulder.

She turned to face him, coming up practically against his chest. "Hi, there." She giggled, and tipped up the brandy bottle, taking a hefty swig. "I hate drinking alone. You have a drink, too."

"I can't afford to. I'm on a job."

She was almost more temptation than he could stand. But he had a responsibility to her. To the mission.

"I want to kiss you," she announced.

"I work for you. It's totally inappropriate."

She reached up, placing a soft hand on either side of his face. "John, you're fired. Now kiss me."

Dear Reader,

From the first time I met John Hollister in *The Medusa Seduction,* I just knew he had to get his own book someday. What I wasn't expecting was the story he whispered into my ear…and then kept whispering at me until I finally agreed to write it down for him. Thankfully, Melina Montez came along, and she was fully up to the daunting task of taking on John and his personal baggage.

This story holds a special place in my heart. I wrote it at a time when both my mother and mother-in-law were fighting cancer. I wanted to write a book for them about the power of love overcoming death and thoughts of death. In many ways, Melina is the two of them. She's a fighter who laughs richly, loves without reservation and lives with gusto. And isn't that, after all, how we all should live every day of our lives?

So to Mom, Mom Dees, and all of you, dear readers, here's to a great read and to a life well lived and well loved!

All my best,

Cindy Dees

Silhouette®

Romantic

SUSPENSE

ISBN-13: 978-0-373-27631-8
ISBN-10: 0-373-27631-1

NIGHT RESCUER

This edition published by arrangement with Harlequin Books S.A.

Visit Silhouette Books at www.eHarlequin.com

Printed in U.S.A.

Books by Cindy Dees

Silhouette Romantic Suspense

**Behind Enemy Lines* #1176
**Line of Fire* #1253
**A Gentleman and a Soldier* #1307
**Her Secret Agent Man* #1353
**Her Enemy Protector* #1417
The Lost Prince #1441
†*The Medusa Affair* #1477
†*The Medusa Seduction* #1494
***The Dark Side of Night* #1509
Killer Affair #1524
***Night Rescuer* #1561

Silhouette Bombshell

Killer Instinct #16
†*The Medusa Project* #31
Target #42
†*Medusa Rising* #60
†*The Medusa Game* #79
Haunted Echoes #101
†*The Medusa Prophecy* #122

*Charlie Squad
†The Medusa Project
**H.O.T. Watch

CINDY DEES

started flying airplanes while sitting in her dad's lap at the age of three and got a pilot's license before she got a driver's license. At age fifteen, she dropped out of high school and left the horse farm in Michigan where she grew up to attend the University of Michigan. After earning a degree in Russian and East European Studies, she joined the U.S. Air Force and became the youngest female pilot in its history. She flew supersonic jets, VIP airlift, and the C-5 Galaxy, the world's largest airplane. She also worked part-time gathering intelligence. During her military career, she traveled to forty countries on five continents, was detained by the KGB and East German secret police, got shot at, flew in the first Gulf War, met her husband and amassed a lifetime's worth of war stories.

Her hobbies include professional Middle Eastern dancing, Japanese gardening and medieval reenacting. She started writing on a one dollar bet with her mother and was thrilled to win that bet with the publication of her first book in 2001. She loves to hear from readers and can be contacted at www.cindydees.com.

Chapter 1

Somewhere in the Caribbean

Major John Hollister, commander of the Wolf Pack, an elite special operations squad for the H.O.T. Watch, highly decorated combat veteran, and the only man ever to lose eight men on a single H.O.T. Watch mission, placed a rickety chair in the middle of the storeroom and stepped onto its wobbly seat. Balancing carefully—*wouldn't want to screw up the maneuver at this delicate juncture*—he flung the end of a heavy rope over the giant log beam overhead. Gotta love these islanders. They knew how to build a heck of a solid building, what with all the hurricanes in this part of the world.

With ease of long experience with ropes, he made a quick hitch knot that secured the rope tightly to the beam. He grabbed the thick hemp in both hands and gave it a good yank. Yup, it would hold his weight.

He grabbed the noose he'd fashioned earlier at the other end of the rope and gave it a long, hard look. This was it. The end. What was a man supposed to think at this final moment of his life, when he was staring his own death square in the face? What was he supposed to feel?

Thing was, he thought nothing. Felt nothing. And that was the problem. John Hollister was an empty shell of a human being. A waste of space on planet Earth. First he screwed up his own life, and then threw away those of his men. Guilty times eight. Yup. Definitely time to check out. He leaned forward to place his neck through the noose. *Just kick the chair away and it will be over.* The whole useless, pathetic mess he'd managed to make of it all.

He started at the cheerful tinkle of a bell out front in the main room of the shipping company announcing that a customer had opened the front door. *Oh, for the love of Mike. Couldn't a guy hang himself around here without someone interrupting him?*

Disgusted at the delay, he hopped down off the chair, landing out of habit in complete, stealthy silence. He stepped out of the storeroom and up to the scarred wooden counter.

"Can I help you?" he asked wearily.

"I certainly hope so."

He looked up, startled at the smooth, dulcet tones of the female voice that answered him. Whoa. The woman who went with all that come-hither velvet lived up to her voice, and then some. She was slender, her skin a delicious caramel color. Her hair would probably be called brown if it weren't streaked with all those golden, sun-kissed blond highlights. Her eyes were light brown and looked right through him to the blackest depths of his soul.

Shockingly, an emotion actually registered in his gut. Embarrassment at what she'd almost caught him doing. He reeled back from her steady gaze, stunned.

"Uhh, what is it you need today?" He pulled himself together enough to ask.

"I need something delivered. Something…unusual."

"That's what we do here at Pirate Pete's Delivery Service. Anything, anywhere."

At the mention of his name, the large green parrot dozing in the corner of the shabby office roused himself on his perch and gave his wings a shake. With a squawk, the bird announced, "*Baawwk.* Pirate Pete is a dirty old bird. Repeats every joke that he's heard. Tells the girls with big tits, which guy licks the best—"

"Quiet, Pete!" John cut him off sharply. That damned bird was forever spouting off some filthy limerick. And always to the attractive female customers, it seemed.

"*Baawwk!*" Pete retorted, clearly offended at the interruption. "John Cowboy is ever so quick, sees a girl and he whips out his—"

"*Pete.* Shut up."

The woman's worried expression gave way to a dazzling, toothpaste-commercial smile that belonged on the big screen. *Wow.*

He mumbled, "Sorry 'bout that. Should've strangled and stuffed that bird a long time ago."

"I think he's cute."

John rolled his eyes. "All the girls say that. I don't know what they see in that feathered old reprobate."

The customer replied, "He's direct. It's refreshing. A girl can relate to it."

The way she was gazing into his eyes was pretty damned direct, too. If he planned on living past the next ten minutes, she would be the kind of woman who would give him serious pause. He cleared his throat. "You said you need something delivered? Where and when?"

"To Peru. As soon as possible."

"Well, we can package it and express mail it for you or, if it's really urgent, we can courier it down there for you. We can have it in Lima late tonight if we take it ourselves."

"Oh, this delivery isn't going to Lima. I'm afraid it isn't that simple. It's going way up into the Andes mountains. I'm told there aren't even roads to the final destination."

No roads? Man, that was remote. "We can fly it in by helicopter or even air-drop your package...but that would be pretty expensive. You might want to consider having us arrange a Peruvian guide to hump your package back into the mountains by llama. It'll take longer to get there, but it won't bankrupt you."

"I'm not worried about money." But the look in her eyes said she was plenty worried about something.

His invisible warning antennae wiggled. Something was up with her. What wasn't she telling him? After almost fifteen years as an army officer, much of it in command positions, he had a finely honed sense of when he wasn't hearing the truth...or in this case, the full truth.

"So when's your drop-dead date?"

The woman started violently. "I beg your pardon?"

He rephrased quickly. "When does your package absolutely have to be there?"

"There's not a set deadline. But the sooner the better."

"In that case, I'd go with letting us fly it to Lima and then handing it off to a Peruvian pack train."

She turned over the plan for a few seconds. Her fawn-colored eyes gazed deeply into his, measuring whether or not he was someone to be trusted. "If you think that's best..."

What the hell. He might as well close the sale before he went in back and finished himself off. He asked smoothly, "What are we delivering, ma'am?"

"Me."

* * *

Navy Commander Brady Hathaway jolted as one of the floor controllers below abruptly barked, "Commander. Come here! We've got a problem."

He descended from the observation deck to the floor of what they fondly called the Bat Cave—a hundred-twenty-yard-long, fifty-foot-high cavern hollowed out millions of years ago by magma from a now extinct volcano. His shoes rang in quick staccato on the steel steps. None of the two dozen computer and surveillance technicians on duty at the rows of consoles took that sharp tone of voice with him lightly. Plus, when Carter Baigneaux—a longtime Special Forces operator himself—said there was a problem, it was guaranteed to be a bona fide crisis.

As Brady's long strides carried him across the floor, the question foremost in his mind, though, was why Carter had told him to come down onto the floor. Why hadn't he sent whatever image had his Cajun knickers in such a twist to one of the big screens on the far wall for everyone to see? Six JumboTrons lined the far wall, at the moment displaying various satellite tracking maps of the world.

He reached the technician's desk and the array of monitors on it. "What've you got?" he asked tersely.

Carter stabbed a finger at his far left monitor. "I was cruising through a routine check of the surveillance cameras in the cave complex and I spotted this upstairs at Pirate Pete's."

Brady took one look at the noose dangling damningly in the middle of the cluttered storeroom. "Who's on duty up there?" he bit out.

"Hollister."

Brady swore violently. He took off running, sprinting across the floor, leaving rows of startled technicians in his wake. He raced down a low tunnel hollowed out of volcanic rock and skidded to a stop in front of the large freight elevator that carried people back and forth between the Bat Cave and Pirate Pete's Delivery Service up on the surface. The decrepit shipping company and its ramshackle office acted as a front for the H.O.T. Watch's surveillance operation here in the Caribbean. It allowed his guys to move around on missions with a credible cover, and it explained to the locals some of the supplies and personnel that came and went from the island.

C'mon, c'mon, he urged the elevator. He knew Hollister was messed up after that last mission, but he'd had no idea the guy was actually contemplating offing himself. Brady shoved a distracted hand through his hair. It hadn't been Hollister's fault. Nobody'd seen the ambush. They'd all been suckered. It had been a miracle that Hollister himself hadn't been killed. The guy'd been shot in the back—it had taken months to heal and he still wasn't cleared to go out on operational Special Forces missions.

The elevator's double doors started to slide open, and Brady turned sideways, jumping into the space before they'd fully opened.

Thank God.

The noose still hung empty from the beam in the middle of the room. The entire storeroom and all its sloppy contents were, in fact, the elevator down to H.O.T. Watch Ops. He opened the rusted electrical panel and punched the button disguised as a circuit breaker that would return him to the surface and Pirate Pete's. As the elevator lurched into silent motion, he climbed up on the chair quickly and untied Hollister's knots. He flung the rope away in distaste.

The storeroom/elevator came to a halt. He heard voices out in the front room. A woman laughed. Ahh. That explained why Hollister hadn't finished off the job, yet. He'd been interrupted by a customer. God bless her.

He took a calming breath and stepped out casually. "Hey, folks."

The woman jumped. Edgy, she was. Hollister jumped, too, and threw a chagrined look past Brady to the storeroom from whence he'd just emerged. Brady ignored him and instead nodded pleasantly at the woman—who was a hell of a looker.

Hollister spoke up. "The lady, here, wants to have herself delivered to a remote area of Peru. She says there are no roads to where she wants to go, and she prefers a ground insertion to an air insertion."

Brady's eyebrows went up. An unusual request. Peru wasn't exactly the safest place on the planet, particularly back in the mountains. Shining Path guerrillas still roamed the region, not to mention various drug growers and runners, and plain, old-fashioned bandits. "That's a pretty dangerous destination. May I ask why you want to go somewhere like that?"

Her expression became closed. Stubborn. She replied smoothly, "It's personal. I really can't go into the details."

"Fair enough. When do you want to leave?"

"As soon as possible."

Brady thought fast. All the shrinks had talked to Hollister. They'd prescribed painkillers and sleeping pills and declared him mildly depressed, but that was to be expected after a traumatic loss like he'd experienced. In private to Brady, the shrinks had declared him ready to return to duty. But Hollister had, as of yet, made no move to get himself removed from the injured reserve list. And something Brady couldn't quite put his finger on didn't seem right with John. He'd hesitated to put his old friend back in the field for a couple of months now.

No matter what the docs said about the guy being ready to get back in the saddle, that noose in the back room shouted otherwise. Like many experienced field operators, Hollister apparently could successfully bullshit a psychiatrist.

Brady tapped his front tooth thoughtfully. The fact remained that he had a suicidal operator on his hands. And if Hollister really wanted to kill himself, there wasn't a whole hell of a lot he was going to be able to do to stop the guy. The problem with men like him and Hollister was they were trained in too many forms of killing. There was really no way to stop them from successfully turning that knowledge on themselves if they so chose.

He eyed the woman before him speculatively. Hollister was a responsible guy. Too responsible. It was the reason he was such a mess now. If he put Hollister in charge of getting this woman safely to her destination, the major would take that responsibility seriously. Enough to stay alive and finish the job. He still might kill himself out in the mountains of Peru after the woman was delivered to wherever she wanted to go, but it might buy Brady a little time to figure out how in the hell to talk Hollister into living. It was worth a shot.

Decision made, he announced, "We'd be glad to take you to Peru, ma'am. Cowboy, here, is just the man to escort you there."

Hollister's gaze jerked to him in surprise and denial. Brady blandly ignored the frown and miniscule negative shake of the head that Hollister threw him.

The woman's gaze swiveled to Hollister. Her mouth curved up into a sudden and blinding smile. "Cowboy? As in John Cowboy?"

Hollister glared over at Pirate Pete in the corner. "That's correct. John Hollister, ma'am. Pleased to meet you."

She held a slender hand across the counter. "Melina Montez."

Brady interrupted smoothly. "Why don't you go over Miss Montez's travel documents with her and figure out what visas and shots and the like she'll need for the trip. In the meantime, I'll have one of the boys bring over your gear, Cowboy."

He damn well wasn't giving John Hollister a second alone until the guy walked out the door with the woman.

Hollister must've figured that out because he sighed in resignation. "Fine. I'll take her to Peru."

But the promise to finish what he'd started in the storeroom hung heavy in his voice. Brady made brief eye contact with his best field commander, sending him a silent plea to reconsider. But the look in Hollister's eyes was firm. Implacable.

The guy'd made his decision and he wasn't budging. Brady might have delayed the inevitable with this little stunt of sending him to Peru, but inevitable it was.

Dammit.

Chapter 2

Melina was a bit shell-shocked at how quickly these two men verified her travel papers, which she'd already secured for Peru. They outfitted her with a backpack and assorted clothing and gear from a local sporting goods store and drove her by Jeep to a long but deserted-looking airstrip. No more than an hour, all told.

The second man—Brady, he called himself—climbed into the pilot's seat of a twin-motor, eight-passenger airplane he called a King Air, while Hollister threw their gear in the back and helped her climb in.

The airplane buzzed down the runway and leaped into the air, bumping through some afternoon turbulence, then settling into a steady drone.

Brady, up front, set some sort of autopilot and leaned back to relax. Hollister slipped out of the copilot's seat and came to sit across the narrow aisle from her.

"Where are we going?" she asked.

"We'll make a fuel stop in Colombia, but then we'll go direct to Lima. It's going to take about eight hours. Go ahead and make yourself comfortable back here. Snacks are in that cupboard and coffee's below it. The boss and I will be up front. If you need anything, just tap on one of our shoulders."

She nodded and enjoyed the view of his broad shoulders and narrow hips as, half crouching, he made his way back into the cockpit. A handsome man he was, with that dark hair and those mysterious gray eyes. Classy. Mature. A certain... sadness…clung to him, though. It made her want to take him in her arms and comfort him.

Her hunky guide disappeared into the cockpit and she leaned her head back against her seat. Finally, she was on her way. She'd both dreaded and wished for this moment to arrive. She was very quickly approaching the point of no return. Once she made contact with Huayar's men, she was committed. They would not let her leave Peru alive. They'd made that very clear when they had contacted her yesterday morning.

It wasn't like she'd had any choice, though. They had her brother Mike and both of her parents, and if she didn't come, they'd all die. Horribly.

She had no illusions about what she was journeying into. It would be terrible beyond imagination. Rough, uncivilized, perhaps cruel. With death likely waiting at the end of it all. She dreaded this trip more than anything she'd ever had to do in her entire life. At least her guide came across as knowing his stuff. Once he'd reluctantly given in to his boss and agreed to do this trip, he'd been all business, focused and efficient. For the moment, she felt safe.

And right now, she was living moment by moment. What lay before her was simply too immense to process all at once. How did that old adage go? A journey of a thousand miles begins with a single step?

Well, she'd taken the first step. The ball was in motion

now. All that remained was for it to gather speed and roll to the inevitable end of the road. Why then, did she feel like throwing up?

Sometime later, a light touch on her shoulder made her start violently awake.

"Easy, Miss Montez. We're in Colombia. You'll have to come inside with me to a Customs holding area while Brady refuels the plane."

She stumbled inside a blindingly bright, antiseptic room with garish, orange plastic chairs. The stagnant, humid air, smelling of too many unwashed bodies, assaulted her. Closing her eyes, she told herself it was the first of many hardships to come. She might as well get used to it.

A warm hand cupped her elbow. "Are you all right?"

She opened her eyes to gaze up into Hollister's concerned gaze. His eyes were a stormy gray that mirrored her emotions. "I'm fine. Why?"

"You went pale all of a sudden."

And he'd noticed? Wow. Observant guy. "The heat in here…and the smell… I'm not used to them."

He frowned faintly. "Are you sure you're up for this journey? It's going to be primitive out there."

"I've got no choice. It has to be done."

"Why's that?"

Her gaze fell away from the penetrating stare he leveled at her. "The less you know, the better. It's a family thing."

"So, you're going to see your family?"

She suppressed bitter laughter and managed to answer dryly, "Something like that."

She was saved from any more questions by an airport employee sticking his head through a door and announcing that their plane was ready to go. A baby-faced Customs official, who looked no more than sixteen, escorted them back out to their airplane and stood there just outside Melina's window until the engines started and they'd taxied out of their parking space.

On to Peru. The second step taken. One step closer to her death.

It was dark when they landed in Lima. Her back was sore from sitting in an airplane seat for so long, and her entire body vibrated with the residual aftereffects of the propellers. She was surprised when Brady handed their backpacks down to her and Hollister but didn't get off the plane.

"Here's where we part company, ma'am. You stick with John. He'll take care of you. There's no better man anywhere."

She smiled up at the pilot and then over at her escort, who was frowning again.

To him, Brady said, "Take care of yourself."

Hollister's frown deepened.

"I mean it," Brady added.

The atmosphere between the two men was thick with something unspoken. Hollister broke the tension by plucking her backpack off her shoulder and turning away from his boss. "C'mon, Miss Montez. Let's get this show on the road."

"Call me Melina."

"If you'll promise not to call me John Cowboy."

She grinned and hurried to keep up with him as they crossed to a low passenger terminal under pink halogen lights.

There was a lengthy delay getting through Customs. The Peruvian soldiers didn't like some of the equipment John had in his bag, and seemed even less impressed by his bland explanation that they were planning on going camping. She was startled that the soldiers didn't end up confiscating any of his gear. The Peruvians were notorious for helping themselves to electronics and gadgets out of tourists' bags. But then, one look at Hollister and she'd think twice about taking anything from him, too. He was big. Powerful. Dangerous-looking. It wasn't so much an expression, but the way he carried himself. He looked...competent. Like he could handle any situation that came his way.

Apparently, the Peruvian Customs officials read him the same way. Eventually, her passport and John's were stamped and they were cleared into the country.

The third step taken. She was getting very close now, to that irrevocable step. She felt it closing in on her like walls collapsing on her head, suffocating her—

"Are you all right?" Hollister asked, concerned. He'd paused in front of the terminal under a streetlight. His big body hovered close, protective. One of his hands came up, landing lightly in the middle of her back, an unconscious offer of support. Warmth spread outward through her from that light touch, awakening nerves that had been far too long asleep. Feelings unfolded in her core that she barely recognized anymore. A feeling of femininity. Of being attractive. Of being attracted. Of mattering to another human being.

Her pulse sped up even more. She was perilously close to panicking. Her head spun and stars danced before her eyes. "Uhh, I'm okay."

"The humidity can get crazy bad here, not to mention the altitude. It may not feel like much at first, but the combination can really sap your energy. You've got to take it easy for a few days until your body adjusts. Try to breathe deeply and slowly."

She nodded and tried to take a deep breath. Best to let him think it was the altitude making her hyperventilate. He was a decent guy. No need to involve him in this fiasco.

In short order, he hailed a taxi and gave the name of a hotel to the driver. His Spanish was effortless, as fluent as hers, and she'd lived in Mexico City for the past eight years. He'd obviously been to Lima before, because he leaned forward and challenged the taxi driver when the guy tried to take an overly circuitous route to wherever they were going. The driver shrugged and grinned and took the route Hollister told him to. Gratitude at not having to deal with these annoying travel details flooded her. It felt great to have someone take care of her for a change.

The building they stopped in front of was built in the classical style; its limestone facade old but elegant. A brass sign announced that this was the Hotel Alvarado. The old-world elegance continued inside.

Hollister stepped up to the counter. "Mr. and Mrs. Taylor. We have a reservation."

They did? When had he arranged that? She masked her surprise. The clerk handed over a key, and Hollister smiled down at her fondly. "C'mon, honey. You look exhausted. Let's get you to bed."

Her gaze snapped to his. To bed with him? As husband and wife? A thrill rippled through her. It had been far too long since she'd even entertained such a thought about any man. His gray eyes went darker and stormier than usual as they registered where her thoughts had obviously drifted. And just as quickly as it had come, the expression disappeared, carefully banked.

She all but rocked backward on her heels. John Hollister was a force to be reckoned with. Definitely not a man to be taken lightly. And she was about to go traipsing into the wilds of South America with him. Alone. A sudden urge to fan herself nearly overcame her.

He spun abruptly on his heel and headed for the elevators. She followed cautiously. They rode up to their floor in silence, the close atmosphere of the tiny space felt charged. He led the way to a brass-numbered door and unlocked it, holding it open for her. She brushed by him, and was startled to catch a whiff of something masculine and expensive. He worked in a ramshackle hut in the Caribbean and wore a designer aftershave? Who *was* he?

The door closed behind her as she stared in dismay at the single, king-size bed dominating the room.

"Don't worry about that. I'll sleep on the floor," he said from behind her. "But it helps us blend in if we appear to be a married couple."

She snorted. Like who she slept with was going to matter for squat in a few weeks. "I don't care if you sleep in the bed. You strike me as the kind of man who'd be a gentleman."

"You consider yourself a good judge of character, do you?" he replied.

She turned to face him. "I've had a couple of colossal misses in my day, but my instincts are usually right."

"What are your instincts saying about me?"

He asked the question casually enough, but all of a sudden thick anticipation hung in the air between them. She studied him closely. No two ways about it. The man was gorgeous. But there was more to him than that. There was the whole competence thing she'd already noticed, but the way he held himself…ramrod straight, dignified…

"My instincts say you are a formidable man, John Hollister."

He cocked an eyebrow and said nothing.

"You're honest. Maybe to a fault. You're—" she searched for a word "—demanding of the people around you."

That made him start a bit. She must have hit a nerve.

"But you're more demanding of yourself. How am I doing so far?"

A shrug. But his eyes had gone nearly black.

"I think you don't laugh nearly enough. You're goal-oriented. Probably don't know how to relax."

"I can relax," he disagreed.

She wagged a finger at him. "Ahh, but do you choose to? I think not."

"How do you come to all these fascinating conclusions about me?"

"Your jaw. It's all there in your jaw."

"My—I thought the window to the soul is the eyes."

"Not in your case. You don't show anything of yourself in your eyes."

"That, I can believe," he muttered. "Thank God."

"Okay. Your turn. What do your instincts tell you about me?" she challenged.

"You don't want to know." And with that, he whirled and headed for the door. "I've got to go out for a little while. There are a few supplies I still need to get for our trip."

Things he couldn't get past the Peruvian Customs officials? Like weapons, maybe? She didn't say anything aloud. Her evasive escort wouldn't have told her anyway, if she didn't miss her guess.

"Stay here," he ordered. "Don't answer the phone and don't let anyone into the room. I'll be back soon."

He slipped out of the room quietly, the door closing silently behind him.

John leaned against the wall of the elevator, breathing hard. Damn, that woman had pegged him cold. How in the world had she done that? For some reason it scared the hell out of him that she could see through him so easily. He was supposed to be a rock. Never show any emotion. Be in complete control at all times. Had he lost his edge completely for a civilian to read him like an open book?

What in the hell was he doing out here? He was in no shape to go on any sort of field operation. But then, this wasn't an actual mission. It was a simple delivery job. Just take the woman to see her family wherever they were tucked away up in the mountains.

Nonetheless, his instincts told him to treat this like a full-blown op. To arm himself and go to ground as if he and Melina were both in mortal danger. And like Melina, his instincts were usually spot-on. Usually. He'd been dead wrong in a cold Afghani mountain pass a few months ago. And his entire team had paid the price. The ultimate price. And here he was, in a swanky hotel with a beautiful woman, alive and kicking, while eight good men—his men—were turning to dust.

He swore and stepped out of the elevator.

Melina stepped out of the shower, having steamed herself to approximately the doneness of a cooked lobster. Out of her original suitcase—the one she'd packed at home, not the backpack Hollister had filled for her on the island—she pulled out a purple lace lingerie ensemble and donned it. Over that she pulled a stretchy black dress that hugged her curves like a fine race car on a fast track. She'd worked off a whole lot of frustrations over her research in the gym over the years, and she might as well show off the results in this, her last hurrah.

She slipped on a strappy pair of black stilettos. She hadn't the slightest idea why she'd packed them, but they were the sexiest shoes she owned, and she'd wanted to have them with her. For confidence. How pathetic was that? She had to turn to clothing for moral support. Where had the brash, smart, ballsy young woman that she'd once been gone? When had she allowed life to turn her into a meek, uninteresting doormat?

A man like John Hollister would never settle for a doormat. Of that she was sure. And maybe that was why she'd donned her little black dress and these shoes. She turned off all the lights before she opened the drapes and sat down in a chair by the window. She'd gotten the impression from the false names at the front desk that Hollister didn't want to advertise their presence in Lima just yet. And frankly, that was fine with her. The longer she delayed making herself known to Huayar's men, the better. They'd close in on her like circling sharks, and then the jig would be up.

How long she sat there in the dark, gazing out at the lights of Lima and the distant, unearthly glow of the moon preparing to rise over the mountains, she didn't know. It was peaceful. It had been a long time since she'd been truly alone like this. She spent almost every waking hour at the lab, surrounded by government officials and guards and the pharmaceutical firm's eager executives, all of them hovering over her work while they waited for her to invent the next designer drug to replace methamphetamine, and in so doing, win a huge government contract to create its antidote.

She started violently when the hotel room door opened behind her. She felt the dark shadow of John Hollister glide into the room on high alert.

"Everything's all right. I was just enjoying the moonrise," she murmured.

A shadow on the far side of the bed straightened into the outline of a man and detached itself from the wall. He moved over behind her chair to look out the window. A golden, glowing ball broke free of the Andes mountains and lifted majestically into the night sky, rapidly growing smaller and whiter as it went.

"Beautiful, isn't it?" she said.

"Yes. It is."

"You sound surprised."

He replied contemplatively, "I don't remember the last time I watched a moonrise."

"Too busy chasing the girls, huh?"

A snort came from behind her. "Something like that."

"Did you get what you need?"

"Yes. We're good to go. When are you supposed to collect the final directions as to where we're heading?"

"As soon as I call to let…my family…know I'm here."

"And why do we need to get these coordinates, again?" he asked lightly.

She answered in an equally light, but wholly false, tone,

"They move around frequently in their work. Once they know when I'm arriving, then they can tell me where they'll be."

"And who, exactly, are we meeting?"

She sighed. "Mr. Hollister—"

"I know. Don't ask." A pause. "Call me John."

Silence fell between them. The moonlight took on a cold, metallic hue that sent a chill across her skin. She rubbed her arms to chase away the sudden goose bumps.

"Hungry?" he finally asked.

"As a matter of fact, I am."

"You're in luck. People eat late in this part of the world. When I came in, it looked like they were still serving in the restaurant downstairs."

He held a hand down to her to help her out of her seat, and she reached up to take it. Their palms touched, and the skies opened around them. Infinite possibility soared overhead, wide open and free, inviting her to come fly. Startled, she looked up at him. His eyes blazed out of the shadows, compelling and full of dark magic. It washed over her, drawing her in and seducing her. She threw herself into the promise of his gaze, succumbing without a whimper. He gave an easy tug on her hand, and she floated to her feet before him.

He sucked in a sharp breath. "Nice dress."

A genuine smile started in her toes and spread upward until it blossomed on her face. "Thanks. Thanks for noticing."

He cleared his throat. "Kinda hard not to. You look… dynamite."

She was going to kiss him if he kept that up. *Kiss.* Now there was a thought. A totally inappropriate one, but my, how tempting. She followed him to the door, feeling wobbly, and not because of the heels.

As the elevator whisked them downward he murmured, "Don't forget we're a couple. You're my woman and I'm your man. Got it?" The door slid open and his hand landed possessively on the back of her neck, his thumb caressing the tender flesh under her hair. The promise of raw, unadulterated sex roared through his fingertips.

She glanced up at him, shock in her eyes.

He nodded, his smile sizzling her all the way to her toes. "Better. That's how a woman about to be made love to until she can't stand up should look."

Her jaw dropped. He led her across the lobby, his hand never leaving her neck, his thumb never stopping that light, possessive caress. Waves of tingling shivered through her, starting at her neck and racing outward in expanding spirals of delight. All the loneliness of the past few years slammed into her full force. How long had it been since a man touched her like that? *If only it were real.* Intense longing nearly brought her to her knees.

As they approached the French doors into the restaurant, she threw him a sidelong glance. "You know, it's not nice to tease. If you're going to say something like that to a lady, you really should mean it."

His retort stole away what little breath she had left. "Who says I don't?"

Chapter 3

John was startled at the effect his words had on her. A shiver raced across her skin, and her eyes went so big and dark he could see all the way to her soul. Distracted, he guided her behind the maître d' to a candlelit table in a dark, secluded corner. John took one look at the table their host had selected for them and a reluctant smile tugged at his mouth. Apparently, the steamy lovers act must be working.

He stepped smoothly in front of the host and held Melina's seat for her, his hand brushing across her bare shoulders as he moved to her right and took the seat that put his back to the wall.

He leaned back, amused, as Melina made a production out of studying the menu as if she were going to have to take a test over its contents. The line of her cheek captivated him. DaVinci couldn't have drawn it more beautifully than Mother Nature had. She really was a stunning woman. Polished as brightly as a fine diamond. If she didn't come from money, and a lot of it, she faked it very well. She seriously didn't strike him as the type to want to run around in the rugged mountains of South America.

She glanced up. "Do you know what you're ordering?"

He nodded. "I'm still deciding how I want my dessert, though."

Her cheeks blossomed twin spots of pink and her chest lifted on a quick breath. Give the lady high marks for catching the subtleties of double entendre.

When the waiter came, Melina exchanged pleasantries with the guy in perfect Spanish before ordering effortlessly in the same tongue. Where did she learn to speak that tongue so well? John wished there'd been time to run a background check on her before they left Pirate Pete's. But Brady Hathaway had been in such an all-fired hurry to hustle him out of there and away from that noose that he'd barely had time to collect his own gear, let alone outfit Melina.

John ordered a steak—rare—salad with vinaigrette, roasted local vegetables, no mushrooms, and a bottle of wine, lightly chilled. The waiter left, and John turned his attention back to his dinner companion. Time to do his own background check. In the guise of polite dinner conversation, of course.

"For an American, you speak Spanish exceptionally well."

"I live in Mexico City."

"What do you do there?"

Her eyes clouded over. "I work for a pharmaceutical company."

She didn't look particularly happy about it, though. They sipped their wine in silence while he considered her. He couldn't come up with a single reason why a cosmopolitan woman like her needed to go on a trek in the Andes that was so obviously not for pleasure. What was she up to?

"Tell me about yourself," he said casually as he refilled her wine glass.

She swirled the maroon liquid, staring down into it pen-sively. She looked up abruptly, her reverie broken. "Why don't you tell me about me? You dodged my question earlier. Let's see how your instincts stack up to mine."

Fine. Maybe he could shake loose some information out of her by playing along. He sipped his wine, studying her until she began to fidget beneath his intent gaze.

Only then did he speak. "All right, here goes. My overall impression of you is that you're generally frustrated."

Her eyebrows shot straight up. Interesting reaction. He expanded on the impression. "You have a decent education that you're either not using or don't like how you're using. You don't like what you're doing with your life. You're not in a satisfying relationship, and perhaps that frustrates you most of all. And well it should. A beautiful, bright woman like you should expect to have a good man in her life."

Storm clouds drifted into her gaze.

"Ahh," he said in realization. "You thought you had a good man, didn't you? But you misjudged him. One of those colossal errors in judgment you mentioned earlier."

A startled look flashed through her expressive eyes. He didn't even need to attempt to read her body language. Her eyes were an open book. He'd hit it spot on. How long ago had that ugly breakup been? She wasn't giving him any clues on that. Could be recent; could be an old wound.

"What else?" she asked cautiously.

"You're hiding something. Something you're afraid of. You think it'll shock me." She opened her mouth, obviously to protest, but he cut her off with a quick wave of his hand. "For the record, you're wrong. Nothing you could say or do will shock me. Believe me. I've seen it all."

She downed a good half-glass of wine in a single gulp. Bingo. Score another direct hit for him.

"Anything else?" she asked, sounding almost afraid of what else he would say.

"Someone has almost got you convinced that you don't deserve the best for yourself."

She nearly dropped her glass of wine at that one. She fumbled the crystal vessel, recovered it, and downed another large gulp of liquid courage.

"Left to your own devices, I bet you like to have fun. To laugh." He glanced down at where her crossed foot peeked out from under the linen tablecloth to his left. His mouth quirked up at one corner and he continued, "Any woman who'd wear a pair of shoes that sexy has a bit of a brazen streak lurking in her. Since you haven't shown any hint of it to me…yet…I can only assume it means you're a fiery one in the bedroom."

Something flashed in her gaze that he hadn't seen so far. Challenge. Humor. The very fire he spoke of. A silent dare to him to find out if he was right or not.

And something flickered deep in his gut in response. A spark he hadn't felt since before…well, before.

Their meal came, and he found himself taking inordinate pleasure in watching Melina eat. She savored every bite as if it were her last. In turn, he found himself enjoying his succulent steak immensely. It was the first time he could remember actually tasting food in a while.

They finished the bottle of wine with their meal. Melina ordered chocolate mousse for dessert and he did the same. He was surprised when she added an expensive, aged armagnac to the order.

"You know brandy?" he asked in surprise.

She smiled. "I used to."

"Some things you never forget."

She nodded. "Like the taste of a fine cognac."

"Or a fine woman," he remarked lightly.

Whether it was the copious alcohol or embarrassment staining her cheeks that rosy color, he couldn't tell.

The sommelier decanted the armagnac for them, and John watched Melina over his snifter while he let his palms bring the liqueur up to proper drinking temperature. She anticipated the taste of the fine beverage with almost sexual intensity. It had obviously been a long time since she drank cognac. What idiot of a man hadn't been giving it to her nightly, just to watch her enjoy herself like this? It was what he would do if she were his.

She raised her snifter to him in silent toast and sipped the dark amber drink. Her eyes drifted closed, reveling in pleasure long denied and deeply savored.

The alcohol esters drifted up to his nose, carrying hints of vanilla, pepper, rose and chocolate. Wow. Give the woman an A+ for her taste in cognac. Delicately, he sipped the liqueur. It was smooth as silk, its round, Monlezun black oak flavor dripping in subtle finesse. He nodded at the waiter, who left the bottle upright on the table. After all, armagnac and cork didn't mix.

In combination with the chocolate mousse, the fine brandy was sensational. If he didn't know better, he'd swear Melina entered a near orgasmic state across the table from him. Hell, he wasn't far behind.

They finished eating in silence and he signed for the meal, putting it on their room tab. He did a double take at the price tag on the bottle of brandy. That was more than he made in a month. And worth every penny.

"Shall we retire to our room?" he murmured.

She smiled, more relaxed than he'd seen her since they'd met. He held her chair for her. She stood up, snagging the bottle of armagnac on her way past the table. Her gait wasn't a hundred percent steady as he draped his arm over her shoulders and guided her out of the restaurant. When in public in South America with a woman this beautiful, it was generally good policy to stake very obvious claim to her. It avoided no end of unpleasant encounters with single males on the prowl. Besides, the lady wasn't complaining. In fact, she leaned into him as if she found his presence reassuring.

He led her into their room and she kicked off her shoes, dangling the bottle of armagnac from her right hand as she moved across the room in the dark toward the windows.

"Leave the lights off, okay?" she asked.

"Okay." He followed her across the room, vividly aware of the bed looming on his left. He actually felt a little lightheaded. With his body mass and metabolism, he usually held liquor like nobody's business. But apparently, mixing a half bottle of wine with the potent brandy had gotten to him a little. Of course, he usually didn't drink on top of the meds he was still taking for his back pain.

She stood in front of the window, silhouetted against the city lights and the night outside. The woman had a body made for sin. He stepped close behind her and looked over her shoulder.

"I never imagined I'd come to this place," she murmured. "And certainly not under these circumstances."

"What circumstances?"

She turned to face him, coming up short practically against his chest. "Hi there," she giggled.

"I think you're a little bit drunk."

"I hope so. I wish I were a lot drunk." And with that, she tipped up the brandy bottle and took a hefty swig.

"A couple more swallows like that and you will be," he cautioned her.

"I hate drinking alone," she announced. "Here. You have a drink."

"I can't afford to get drunk. I'm on a job."

"There's nothing to do until I call the number they gave me."

She was almost more temptation than he could stand. But he had a responsibility to her. To the mission. To...hell, he didn't know what to... That brandy was damned strong. He felt its effervescence rising to his head, scattering his thoughts.

"Drink." She put the bottle to his mouth and tipped it up. He swallowed a big gulp before he could disarm her of the bottle.

"Easy, darlin'."

"I want to kiss you," she announced.

If she'd sounded a little more drunk, he'd have laughed off the announcement. But as it was, he thought he heard an undercurrent of real intent in her voice.

"I work for you. It's totally inappropriate."

She reached up, placing a soft hand on either side of his face. She looked deep into his eyes, her face wreathed in moonlight and shadows. "John, you're fired. Now kiss me."

He couldn't help it. He laughed. And he was lost. Her laughter rose up to mingle with his, and she took the short step forward, closing the gap between them. She must've stood on tiptoe because her lips nuzzled his ear, sending lust roaring through him.

She murmured, "You think you can make love to me until I can't stand up, huh? This I have to see."

Holy— His brain tumbled like a fighter jet shot down out of the sky and falling wildly out of control toward oblivion. If he were going to be around long enough to have a real relationship with a woman like her, he'd never contemplate making love to her now. He'd get to know her better. Woo her. Let her know he cared about her for more than sex. After all, he was no raw boy intent only on getting a cheap lay.

But hell. As soon as he delivered her to wherever she was going, he was checking out for good. She seemed to be celebrating some sort of unspoken last hurrah, too. Why shouldn't he take her up on the offer? She was an adult, after all. Not to mention beautiful. And sexy. And attracted to him. Hell, she'd initiated it.

How did that old saying go? He who hesitates is lost?

While he hesitated, she reached up and pushed her dress's spaghetti straps off her shoulders. And then, holy mother of God, she pushed her dress down to her waist. The scrap of lace that passed for her bra did more to reveal than cover, and all coherent thought deserted him. He stared, dumbfounded as she shimmied all the way out of the dress, revealing a—sweat popped out on his forehead—lacy thong that was possibly the sexiest thing he'd ever seen.

And he was well and truly lost.

She stepped out of the circle of black fabric on the floor and reached behind her back with both hands for her bra hooks. He stepped forward quickly, reaching around her to stop her hands. "Hey. That's my job."

She laughed up at him, "Well, get to it, then."

"You can't tell me what to do anymore. You fired me."

"Please get to it, then?" She smiled up at him.

He bent his head down to capture all that unleashed joy suddenly bursting from within her. It was as if a floodgate had opened. She'd been so serious, so restrained. But now that she'd let loose, she'd completely let loose. This was the woman he'd sensed beneath her worried, drawn exterior. The real Melina.

But he'd been wrong about her. She wasn't fiery in the bedroom. She was a volcano. In full eruption. Sex appeal not only rolled off her skin until it all but scalded him to touch her, it created a cloud of steam around them that incinerated him from the lungs out. He couldn't get enough of her. He breathed her in, wrapping her in his arms, drawing her satin body up against his. Skin. He wanted to feel her skin with his. He reached for the top button of his shirt and she pushed his hands aside, all but ripping the garment off him.

His belt slithered from around his waist, and her hands were on his zipper in a trice. He sucked in his stomach, frantic to avoid her touch long enough to get naked before he totally lost control. "Slow down, honey. We've got all night."

"It won't be long enough for all I want to do with you," she panted back.

He laughed, but even to his ears it sounded more like a possessive growl. Her palms slid around his waist to the small of his back, pressing him against her. Her breasts pushed impudently against his chest, and his erection pushed even more impudently against his zipper. And his control snapped.

He swept her off her feet and carried her over to the big bed. He followed her down to the cool sheets, lost in her sexual eruption. He had little recollection of how the rest of their clothes came off, but it involved her pushing him onto his back and crawling all over him, and his hands roaming all over her spectacular body while she moaned with need and pleasure.

They should use protection, but he wasn't going to be around long enough to care about his own health. Nonetheless, out of respect for her, he drew back. "Hold on. I've got condoms in my pack."

She pulled him back down to her. "Don't worry about it. It doesn't matter to me."

"I insist. For your safety."

She laughed bitterly. "I'm *so* not safe, you have no idea."

His eyebrows shot up. She corrected hastily. "I don't have any contagious diseases. I swear." As he continued to hesitate, she added, "As I understand it, a person has to actually have sex now and then to get a sexually transmitted disease."

That shot his eyebrows straight to his hair line. A woman of this passion, and she didn't have sex on a frequent and regular basis? It was practically a crime!

Then she was kissing him again. And the lady could kiss like nobody's business, her whole body getting into the act. She made a swear-to-God *purring* noise in the back of her throat. It rippled through him like the ground shock of an explosion, rocking him to his core.

And then her mouth was on his stomach, contracting his

muscles so hard they hurt. He withstood it as long as he could, and then he surged up over her, returning the favor. Her flat stomach went soft and hard by turns under his mouth, her long fingernails raking through his hair in desperate pleasure.

And then she cried out sharply, her entire body trembling. The smell of her pleasure wrapped around him sweet and warm, brandy and chocolate. She drew him up the sinuous length of her body.

"Please, John. I want all of you. And you can have all of me in return."

"I never could refuse a lady," he murmured.

She all but sobbed in relief against him, her slender legs wrapping tightly around his hips. He sank down into her, body and soul, his gaze locked on hers as their bodies became one. Her eyes went wide with delight, fluttering closed on a sigh of pleasure he felt all the way to her core. Almost dizzy with the intensity of her reaction to him, he strained toward her, reaching higher and higher with her. His raw cries joined hers as they built a tsunami between them and rode it like a pair of death-defying big wave surfers.

She pushed on his shoulders, and he rolled onto his back, taking her with him to straddle him even more deeply. He groaned at the sensation. She rocked experimentally, then burst into laughter and rode him with abandon. He clenched his teeth, restraining himself by the thinnest thread.

"You're killing me," he ground out.

She threw her head back. "But what a way to go."

His laughter mingled with hers as he sat up, gathering her in his arms, their bodies still one. She looped her arms around his neck, gazing deep into his eyes. The laughter faded from her expression, and something…unnamed…passed between them.

A moment of naked and total understanding. Of having found a kindred soul. Of seeing past all the artifice, all the emotional defenses, all the petty facades, to the bare truth of one another. Had it been any other moment but this one, they might have recoiled, might have looked away, might have attempted to hide from each other. But as it was, he surged up deep within her and her internal muscles gripped him even more tightly.

He groaned, and she laughed, and the wave of their lovemaking came crashing down upon them, racing up onto shore, tumbling them in its joyous chaos, depositing them upon the sands of a pleasure so intense neither of them could move, let alone stand up. The wave retreated slowly, leaving in its wake a sparkling diamond mist of joy hanging in the sunlight of their souls.

He collapsed onto his back, dragging her down on top of him. She sprawled, satisfyingly boneless, across his insanely sated body. He tingled from the top of his spinning head to the burning soles of his feet.

"Wow," she breathed. "Double wow."

He chuckled. "Triple wow."

She lifted her head languidly, and a shaft of moonlight caught her hair, turning it to spun gold as it draped over her shoulder to tickle his chest. "Wanna do that again?"

"And again, and again, and again."

"Only four times? I thought you looked like you're in better shape than that."

He laughed up at her. "Don't tempt me. The night is young."

"Hah. I dare you."

He narrowed his gaze in a mock scowl. "Thing is, I need you to be able to walk sometime in the next week. Sorry, honey, but I'm going to have to restrain myself."

Her fingernails raked across his chest just hard enough to make him flinch. They trailed down his side and across his hip. "Restrain this," she murmured.

His willing body leaped to attention with surprising alacrity.

"Mmm. That's more like it," she murmured.

"The woman is a wildcat. What have I gotten myself into?"

"You have no idea," she replied, abruptly serious. "I'll do my best to keep you out of it, though. I promise."

He rolled over, pinning her beneath him. "You'll do no such thing. I'm involved with you now, whether you like it or not." They'd looked into each other's souls, for crying out loud. They were most definitely in this together. Whatever *this* was.

Chapter 4

Melina woke up to bright sunlight the next morning, and the oddest sensation under her faintly aching head. Her ear rested on something warm and resilient and suspiciously like a…

She sat bolt upright. Her suspicion had been correct. It was a muscular, and very male, shoulder. And it belonged to John Hollister. It *hadn't* been a dream. A wonderful, incredible, spectacular dream. A perfect night.

Well, at least she'd managed one perfect night before she checked out of the ol' mortal coil. She supposed that was something to be pleased about. John shifted beside her and she glanced down. She was startled to see gray eyes gazing steadily back at her, clear and fully alert. No hangover for him, no sir.

"How're you feeling this morning?" he asked with a distinct note of caution in his voice.

She smiled down at him. "A little dehydration headache, but nothing a couple aspirin and some water won't take care of."

"I have some good painkillers if the aspirin doesn't work,"

he mentioned as he sat up, pooling the sheet in his lap. My, my, my. The man had acres of muscles her anatomy textbooks couldn't have rendered any better.

She shrugged. "I never do anything stronger than aspirin."

"Lucky you. In my line of work, I end up taking all kinds of stuff to keep going. Or at least I used to."

And what line of work would that be, exactly? It occurred to her that he'd drawn quite a bit of information out of her last night but had failed to reciprocate with even the sketchiest details of his life. The sum total of what she knew about him was that he worked for a private courier company, he knew where to pick up a weapon in Peru, and he was positively unbelievable in bed. She'd never been with a man even remotely like him. He made the rest of them seem like adolescent boys fumbling their way through the act.

He swung his feet out of the bed and strolled, gloriously and unconcernedly naked, into the bathroom. Now that was a view a girl could get used to.

"Wanna shower first?" he called out to her.

A slow smile spread across her face. In for a penny, in for a pound. She got out of bed and strolled equally as naked to the bathroom. "How 'bout we share the hot water?"

As she rounded the corner, he looked up from a handful of pills, startled. "Uhh, okay. Lemme get these down."

She stepped forward, curious. "What are those?"

"Carisoprodol."

"A high-powered muscle relaxant? For what?" she asked.

Now, he looked really surprised. "How do you know what carisoprodol does?"

"I work for a pharmaceutical firm, remember?"

"Doing what?"

"Research, mostly."

"What kind of research?"

The kind she emphatically didn't want to talk about. She

replied lightly, "The medical kind, mostly." She stepped over to the shower's water spigot. "Do you like it cool or screaming hot?"

He stepped up behind her and wrapped his arms around her waist. He murmured in her ear, "The more screaming, the better, darlin'."

Laughing she stepped into the shower with him and forgot all about carisoprodol. That was until she moved around behind him to soap up his back. The circular, puckered scar just to the left of his L-4 lumbar vertebra was impossible to miss. Still red, the scar was obviously less than a year old. And was just as obviously a bullet wound.

"Your last girlfriend shot you, huh?" she remarked as she sudsed up the scar.

He started like he'd forgotten it was back there. His back muscles bunched into rock hard ridges of…of what? Embarrassment? Stress? Denial? She couldn't read him at all. A need to comfort him surprised her. She wasn't usually the maternal kind, and John didn't strike her as the kind of man who needed or appreciated being mothered. He was an adult in charge of his own life all the way.

The least she could do was distract him from his scar since she was the one who brought it up. She slid around in front of him, rubbing her slippery, soapy body against his as she went. "Mmm. Nice," she murmured, smiling up at him.

"You're a beautiful woman, Melina Montez," he murmured back. He slicked her hair back from her face, studying her seriously. "Not that many women look this good with their hair wet and no makeup."

"You obviously are blinded by the soap in your eyes," she replied, laughing.

"I may be blinded, baby, but it isn't soap doing the job."

How could a girl resist a compliment like that? She melted against him, savoring the unbearably sensual slide of soapy skin on skin. She stood on tiptoe and wrapped her right leg around his hips in blatant invitation. With the hot water pounding down on them both, he stared down at her, abruptly serious.

"I don't deserve you," he said.

She barely heard him over the sound of the water. "You don't deserve me?" she echoed. "I think you've got that backward. I don't deserve you."

"Ahh, honey, you have no idea. The things I've done—"

The back of her calf rubbed against that telltale scar on his back as she blinked up at him through the shower's spray. "We're both adults. Everyone who hasn't lived in a cocoon has baggage of some kind. I won't hold the skeletons in your closet against you if you won't hold mine against me."

Doubt flickered in his gaze and his eyes glazed with distant thoughts. Was he skeptical of her past or his?

She leaned into him, forcing him to acknowledge her presence. "We're here together now. No past. No future. Just this moment."

He didn't quite come back to her, his eyes were still dark and haunted.

"Come back to me, John," she murmured. She reached down with her hand to guide him into her throbbing heat. Oh, yeah. That did it. Awareness of her roared back into his eyes, and he aggressively took charge of the moment. Wrapping one arm around her waist, he picked her up and backed her against the cool, tile wall of the shower. With his other hand braced by her head, he drove into her until all thought fled her mind. There was nothing at all except the moment and the two of them, the pounding water and steam, and the rhythm of their bodies slapping into one another as they drove away their demons.

They ordered room service and ate in, lazily watching the morning fog burn off the city skyline below. As hard as she tried to ignore it, the moment came when she could no longer delay the inevitable. She had to make that phone call. So much for her fantasy tryst before she handed herself over to the jackals. Her mouth set grimly, she dug in her purse and fished out the piece of paper with the phone number she'd been given to call when she got here. She reached for the telephone.

A big hand landed gently on top of hers, stopping her from lifting the handset. "I'll make the call, Melina."

"They won't talk to you. They're expecting me!"

His gaze narrowed far too intelligently. "Who's *they?*"

"The people I'm supposed to call," she replied with desperate calm. He mustn't mess this up! Her family's lives rode on it. Huayar had been clear. Any deviation at all from her instructions, and her family would be tortured and possibly killed.

"I'm sorry, honey. I need you to be more specific than that."

"John, let me make the call. Please just stay out of this."

He turned at that, capturing both of her hands in his and drawing her away from the phone entirely. He led her across the room and gently forced her down into one of the armchairs. Alarmingly, he continued to stand, looming over her with his arms crossed.

"With all due respect, sweetheart, what the hell's going on? I already told you that you can tell me anything. And I meant it. But I need to know what I'm up against, here."

"You're not up against anything. I hired you to deliver me and nothing more."

He replied dryly, "As I recall, you fired me last night."

She glanced up at him, startled. Humor danced in his silver gaze. "That's not fighting fair to throw that in my face now."

"I never said I fight fair."

She sighed. "John."

"Melina."

"I can't tell you, okay? There's more going on here than meets the eye. But you don't need to know the details. In fact, you'll be safer if you don't know anything."

She scooted backward as he leaned toward her, planting his hands on the arms of the chair and forcing her to arch back to look at him. His expression went blacker than sin. He gritted out words slowly, enunciating clearly. "Whether you like it or not, and whether you cooperate or not, my job is to deliver you to your family safe and sound. If you won't tell me what I'm up against to make that happen, then we're not leaving this hotel room."

"But I have to go…I can't stay here…."

"I'm bigger than you, Melina, and trust me, I'm meaner than you are. We go nowhere until you spill your guts."

She closed her eyes in frustration. And everything had been going so well, marching along exactly according to plan—to Huayar's plan. Maybe John had a point. Maybe taking a modicum of control of this process wouldn't be a bad thing for her. If nothing else, it might alleviate a little of her sense of being a lamb toddling along docilely to her own slaughter.

"Fine," she huffed. "I'm not going to meet my family exactly. It's a work related thing. I'm going to meet some people…to…exchange some information."

"In the remotest region of Peru? What the hell kind of information requires that sort of meeting place?"

She folded her arms stubbornly. "I'm not saying any more. I've already said too much."

He studied her speculatively for long enough that she developed a nearly uncontrollable urge to squirm. Finally, he commented, "I can think of about two innocent reasons for you to be heading deep into the Andes and about ninety-five reasons that are anything but innocent. Which is it?"

They'd made love until the wee hours of the morning last night, had bared their bodies and their souls to one another. He'd looked into the face of her desperation and naked despair and he hadn't flinched. And he didn't strike her as the judgmental type. He gave off a vibe of having done enough things he wouldn't want others to judge, so he wouldn't be the first one to cast stones. Still, she couldn't tell him the truth. And yet, she couldn't bring herself to lie to him, either. That would be too easy, the coward's way out. She pressed her lips firmly together.

He sighed. "Give me the phone number. I'll make the call."

"I already said you can't."

"And I already said you're not doing it. That leaves only me to make the call. End of discussion."

She glared up at him. "Has anyone ever told you that you're a stubborn, unreasonable man?"

"They usually say I'm pigheaded and arrogant, too. But I'll give you a few days to get there. In the meantime, please hand over the phone number nicely, or I may have to take it by force."

"You wouldn't!" she gasped, aghast.

He raised a sardonic eyebrow and merely stared at her. His expression gave away absolutely nothing. Did she believe him, or should she call his bluff? She studied him for a moment more. Nope. He wasn't bluffing. Calm readiness radiated from him. He was fully prepared to mug her for the phone number. Man. She could see where the pigheaded and arrogant accusations came from. Disgruntled, she passed over the slip of paper.

"Thank you," he said with quiet dignity.

Damn him. He would have to go and be a gracious winner, too. That made it harder to stay mad at him. She sat back in her chair with a huff.

He dialed the number quickly.

His end of the conversation was painfully brief and in brisk Spanish. He jotted down something on the pad of paper beside the phone, and then, without asking any questions, got off the phone.

"What did they say?" she cried. "Where are we going? When do we have to be there? Is…everything…okay?"

"Whoa, there, Mel. Slow down."

She reeled back, stunned. Her father was the only person who'd ever called her Mel. Her sweet, absentminded father, whose life hung in the balance. Tears stung her eyelids and she blinked them away rapidly. All of a sudden, John was there, his strong arms wrapping around her and pulling her close. His hand pushed her head down gently onto his shoulder. She drew a sobbing breath. Another. And then she pulled herself together by main force. As much as she wanted to let it all go, she didn't have the luxury. Not yet. Precious lives rode on her keeping her act together. Just a little longer, and then she could lose it.

He leaned away from her, studying her without turning her loose.

"What?" she mumbled.

"You're a strong woman, I'll grant you that. But you're not strong enough to do this alone. You need someone. Let me help you."

"I am letting you help—whether I want to or not," she replied a little peevishly. "You stole the phone number and talked to my contacts, and now you know where to go and I don't."

He nodded slowly. "Good point. And I think I'm going to keep it that way, too. I'm sorry, honey, but I don't entirely trust you not to dump me once we get up in the mountains. I don't know what you're tangled up in, but I damned well know you're in way over your head."

She stared at him, her jaw hanging open. He wasn't going to tell her where they were going? But it was *her* trip. He was just along to act as a guide and travel companion!

"When do you want to leave?" he asked casually.

"Oh, *now* you're asking for my opinion?" she retorted with light sarcasm.

He smiled serenely at her. "No need to get bitchy. This arrangement is for the best and you know it. You're grown-up enough to admit it."

His bland comment stopped her in her tracks. He was exactly right. She was an adult. She wasn't going to lose her cool. She'd traveled thousands of miles and was only days from making a deal with one of the deadliest snakes on the planet. She had bigger fish to fry. As much as she'd enjoy drinking more cognac and hiding from reality with him for a few more days, duty—and her family—called.

She sighed. "I want to leave right away."

He nodded. "Okay, then. Let's dump that ridiculous stuff you packed and then hit the road. We can drive the first part of the trip, but as you suggested, the last part of it's going to have to happen on foot."

She lifted her eyebrows. "Which part of my clothing last night did you find ridiculous? The slinky black dress you couldn't take your eyes off of all the way through supper, or the sexy shoes that made you think naughty thoughts while you were sipping your cognac, or maybe my purple lace bra? Oh, I know. It was that thong you couldn't wait to peel off of me."

He threw up his hands in surrender. "Uncle, uncle! You can take your sexy clothes with you. Let's have a look at what else you've got in your bags and we'll see what we can lose to lighten the load."

As it turned out, most of her non-clothing items—things she'd thought would be vital on a mountain trek—John deemed worthless. It was depressing that she was so unprepared for what lay ahead. But by the same token, he seemed to know precisely what he was doing. Gratitude for his competent presence flooded her yet again…even if he was a bully.

It took them nearly an hour to sort through her luggage and box up the stuff she wouldn't need. John carried it down to the concierge, who promised to mail it to her home in Mexico City. She didn't have the heart to tell John that she wouldn't be needing any of it again. Ever. What he didn't know truly wouldn't hurt him.

She waited impatiently in their room until he secured a vehicle—a banged up Land Rover that might once have been white, but was now permanently stained a dusty beige. She was startled when he hustled her out to a loading dock behind the hotel where he'd parked the vehicle, but she had faith he had a reason for his caution.

She said nothing as he efficiently guided the Land Rover through the squalor and urban sprawl of Lima's suburbs. Eventually, he turned the vehicle onto a two-lane, potholed road that apparently passed for a highway in this part of the world. Lima fell behind, and verdant farmland stretched out around them, terraced up the hillsides.

"What did the guy on the phone say?" she finally broke down and asked John.

"Not much. Just that you were to proceed to a set of coordinates and await further instructions."

"That's all? No...other messages?"

"What sort of message?" he asked smoothly.

"Never mind."

They drove on in silence for a while.

Out of the blue, John said, "He said everyone's fine, so far."

She sagged in her seat, so relieved she felt like crying. The only thought that went through her head, over and over and over was, *Thank God my family's safe.* For now.

And then John asked grimly, "So, tell me. Why would some guy feel compelled to let you know someone is fine? This someone wouldn't be fine why?"

She winced. That was the question of the hour, wasn't it? Bucking up her courage, she looked him in the eye and shook her head regretfully. His eyelids flickered in reluctant acknowledgement. It wasn't a surrender, but it was a declaration of a momentary truce. She'd take it.

She would not...could not...answer his questions. She hadn't the slightest doubt that to do so would spell a death sentence for her parents and her brother. Even if refusing to answer John's questions spelled the end between the two of them, she wouldn't sacrifice her family's safety for her own personal gratification. Ever.

But in the meantime, she had a very curious and increasingly insistent problem on her hands. And it was named John Hollister.

Chapter 5

The drive—a bone-jarring affair that all but rattled Melina's teeth loose—took most of the afternoon. John finally pulled into a gas station in a tiny, impoverished village as the sun began to go down. The hamlet, tucked into a valley lined with green pastures and herds of cattle and alpacas, looked like an old Western movie set with its dusty streets, rust-stained stucco cantina, and a few decrepit vintage cars parked along raised wooden sidewalks.

John opened the door and climbed out. He peeled a few bills out of his wallet and passed them to a wizened, dark-haired man who came outside to pump their gas.

"Stay in the car," John murmured through the window in English.

She sighed. Her legs felt like prickly rubber. She was really ready to get out and stretch. But there'd been a certain tone in John's voice, a warning that he didn't like something about this place. She studied the one-street village out the window, trying to spot what was bothering him. Nothing moved. All was quiet—as in completely deserted. The locals were probably at home by now settling down to supper with their families.

She heard John ask the gas station attendant about the condition of the roads ahead and how far it was to the next village. But she didn't hear the man's mumbled answers. John climbed back in the car and made a production of stowing his wallet and settling into his seat again. As he did so, he said without moving his lips, "We have a decision to make."

"Do tell."

"This place is entirely controlled by whomever you're trying to hook up with. Frankly, I don't think it's safe for us. We can stop here for the night, or we can move on and try to find a village that's neutral territory."

"Did the guy on the phone tell us to stop here?" she asked in an undertone.

John shook his head as he latched his seat belt. "Nope. He said this place was about halfway to where we were going and mentioned that it has an inn, though."

She glanced outside. "Really?" I don't see one."

The gas station attendant said the pub has a couple rooms for rent."

Melina grinned over at him. "For rent by the hour, or the night?"

He grinned back. "I hesitate to think of the state of the bed linens."

She nodded. "We go on."

"I can't promise the next village will be any better," he warned.

She shrugged. "I'm learning to enjoy not playing by the rules. Let's do our own thing tonight."

He grinned over at her. "I like the sound of that."

They drove for another hour as the sun set behind them and twilight settled outside. When the hills had turned a colorless gray and the trees were black silhouettes looming over the road, John exhaled in what sounded for all the world like disgust.

"What's up?" she asked quickly, picking up on his disquiet.

"Traveling at night in this part of the world is asking for trouble."

That didn't answer her question. What wasn't he telling her? She pressed. "What kind of trouble?"

He shrugged and glanced at her. "Pick your poison. Anything from roaming wild pigs to Shining Path guerrillas."

"The way I hear it, they're not so different."

John laughed. "I dunno. Those pigs are pretty smart."

The lightness of the moment faded along with the last vestiges of twilight. She asked soberly, "So what are our options?"

"Here's the thing. The guy in the last village lied to me. He said the next town was forty kilometers away. No more than an hour down this road. We've gone sixty-five kilometers, and there's no sign of civilization anywhere near here."

Alarmed, she blurted, "What does that mean?"

"I imagine our friend has called ahead to some sort of welcoming committee who'll be out here looking for us before too much longer."

Melina jolted, looking around outside, wildly.

"Easy, darlin'. We're far from defenseless. I've got a few aces up my sleeve."

Just then he gripped the steering wheel tightly and swore under his breath. She peered up ahead and made out some sort of large, irregular obstruction lying across the road. It looked like a fallen tree.

"Looks like it's time to pull out one of those aces," she bit out.

"Climb in the backseat," John ordered tersely. "Hurry."

She complied with alacrity, falling in an ungainly heap on top of something hard and sharp in his gear bags.

He continued, "In my green duffel that you're lying on, pull out the big gun on top and a couple of pistols, and pass them up here. Then buckle yourself in back there. We're going cross-country. It's gonna get rough."

He wasn't kidding. He swerved hard to the left, off the road. They banged down and up again through some sort of ditch, and then they took off across an open field strewn with stands of trees and brush. In a matter of seconds, the Land Rover was bucking and bumping over the most god-awful terrain she could imagine. John fought the steering wheel like it was a wild bronco, muscling it forward by sheer force of will. It was an impressive display of strength.

Apparently, the field was some sort of drainage or flood zone, for it was streaked by gullies. Thankfully the gashes, varying in size from a few feet deep to large enough to swallow the entire Land Rover, were mostly dry at the moment. Mostly. Mud splashed up, covering the vehicle's windows until Melina could barely see outside.

A crack of sound, like a truck backfiring, made her jump.

"Get down!" John yelled, flooring the accelerator.

The ride went from horrendous to epic in its discomfort. Amusement park rides had nothing over the pounding she was taking back here! She lay down in the backseat for a few moments, but got so sick so fast that she had to sit up again. She braced a hand against the ceiling to protect her head from banging into the metal roof. How John could see where he was going, she had no idea. It was pitch-black outside, and he'd turned off the headlights. A few more cracks sounded, from behind them this time. She thought she heard faint shouts, but she couldn't be sure.

After a few minutes, the ride smoothed out some, which was to say it went back to merely terrible. A splash of water slammed the window beside her, startling her badly. However, it also washed most of the sticky mud off the window. They were running along the bed of a river-size gully, a high clay wall looming outside the window. Periodically, they crashed into pockets of standing water, some as deep as the front fenders. But the sturdy Land Rover plowed right through them.

Eventually, the vehicle slowed down. John began peering outside, obviously looking for something.

"Can I help? What are we looking for?" she asked breathlessly.

"A low spot in the bank so we can get out of here."

Lovely. They were trapped down in this canyon? What if it ran out on them? Then what? "You're sure no one's following us?" she asked quickly.

"I'm fairly certain they've given up by now. None of them have vehicles with the suspension this one has. They'd be hard-pressed to keep up with us."

"Thank God."

"You can come up here if you like. The ride's smoother than back there, over the rear axle. But you'll have to hold the guns in your lap."

In immense relief, she climbed back into the front seat, managing to get all tangled up in her own legs and arms and seat belts and gun straps. But eventually, she got it all sorted out. She glanced over at John and he was grinning at her.

"What?"

"Having fun yet?" he asked lightly.

"Fun? Fun! You think fleeing armed bandits is *fun*?" she exclaimed.

"Nah, that's just another day at the office. Watching you try to climb into a seat full of firearms—now that's fun."

She stuck her tongue out at him. And realized, suddenly, that he'd effectively broken her tension. She'd bet he hadn't done that by accident, either. "What's next, assuming we can get out of here?"

He shrugged. "We'll get out eventually. It's just a matter of how dicey the maneuver will be. After that, we'll find someplace to hunker down for the night. In the morning, we'll figure out where we are and proceed toward our destination from there."

He made it all sound so easy. She shuddered to think what would have happened to her back there if he hadn't been with her. She'd have driven straight into that ambush. And she had no illusions about how a good-looking, relatively wealthy, foreign woman would have faired at the hands of a bunch of bandits.

"Bingo."

She jumped at John's sudden outburst. He slammed on the brakes and backed the Land Rover up, turning it ninety degrees to face the riverbank on their left. A solid wall of dirt loomed in front of them. "You don't expect to drive up that, do you?" she asked in dismay.

"Sure. No problem."

"That's a vertical wall! We'll flip over."

"Nah, this is a tough old bird. It'll climb that. Hang on, and lean forward when we hit the wall."

Oh my God. She grabbed the bar across the dashboard in horror as he gunned the motor and the Land Rover leaped at the riverbank. The vehicle bucked and slid, its tires clawing at the bank, finding purchase, slipping, then finding purchase again. The vehicle did, indeed, stand up almost on its hind end as the engine roared and the tires threw mud wildly in every direction.

"Lean forward!" John yelled.

She flung herself forward in her seat and John did the same. Whether or not it helped, she had no idea, but at the last moment before she thought the Land Rover had to flip over on its back, its rear wheels caught, and it surged up the last six feet or so of the bank. It burst up and over the edge, skidding sideways as it hit level dirt and the squealing tires caught solid ground.

John stopped the vehicle. He peeled his fingers carefully from around the steering wheel. She noticed they were clawed from the effort and took several seconds to straighten once more. "Well," he panted. "That was fun. You okay over there, Mel? You look a little pale around the gills."

"Near-death experiences have that effect on me," she replied dryly.

He grinned and put the vehicle into gear once more. Driving at a much more sane pace, he eased across the wide pasture they found themselves in. A farmhouse blinked with light on the mountainside above them, but John gave it wide berth and drove past it. On the other side of the dwelling, he let out a quiet exclamation of satisfaction.

She peered outside to see what so pleased him. A dirt road stretched away in front of them. Little more than a parallel pair of gravel tire tracks, it was, nonetheless, a vast improvement over the past half hour's worth of terrain. She sighed in relief as he guided the Land Rover along the crude road.

"Well. That was interesting," she commented.

"More interesting than I was hoping for, but not as interesting as I expected," he replied calmly. What kind of work had he been in before this, that nearly dying at the hands of bandits had barely fazed him? And the way he'd handled the Land Rover—no normal person could've done that. He had some special sort of training. Had he been a policeman, maybe? It would explain his familiarity with guns, too.

"Who were those guys back there?" she asked.

He glanced over at her grimly. "I was hoping you could tell me."

"I don't have any idea!"

He sighed. Brought the Land Rover to a stop. Turned off the ignition and lights. Alarmed, she saw him studying her in the dark, his eyes no more than shadowed hollows of blackness in the night. "True confessions time, Melina. Someone just tried to kill us, and that changes the rules of this game. It means you owe me the full truth and nothing but the truth. Now."

She closed her eyes in despair. "I'm sorry," she whispered.

"Sorry we got shot at, or sorry that you didn't tell me everything up front?" he prodded.

"Both."

A pause stretched out between them until it became awkward. Still, he waited, some of that stubborn pigheadedness of his apparently kicking in. There was no help for it. She absolutely wasn't going to answer his question. She jumped when he abruptly got out of the vehicle and walked around in front of it toward her side of the car. Cringing, she waited as he jerked her door open. She was surprised when he merely held a hand out to her to help her out of the car. She'd pegged him for bodily dragging her out of the vehicle in his current state of irritation.

But he did back her up against the side of the Land Rover in no uncertain terms, his hands on either side of her shoulders, trapping her in place. "What the hell's going on, Melina?"

"What's your gut telling you?" she asked lightly. It was a feeble attempt to remind him of the closeness they'd shared back in the hotel—okay it was a blatant attempt to distract him by reminding him of the great sex they'd had in Lima.

He considered her for several seconds in stony silence. Then he surprised her by answering. "Remember those two legitimate reasons I thought of for you coming out here to meet someone?"

She nodded.

"I think we've pretty much ruled those out as possibilities."

She couldn't help but smile. But as he continued, her humor evaporated.

"Which means you're up to no good. You're out here to meet someone on the wrong side of the law. Very much on the wrong side of the law, or you wouldn't be having to jump through these hoops to even make contact with them. I can only think of a few people who qualify as that criminal and that cautious. And I gotta say, babe, every last one of them is a heaping bad problem."

He continued grimly. "You're dragging me around on a wild-goose chase out here, which tells me your criminal contacts don't trust you. They're vetting you out before they close in on you. So, I'm thinking you either have something you want to sell—" at that, his gaze raked coarsely down her body "—or you're being blackmailed."

She had to work to keep her face from showing anything, either the hurt at his insinuation that she'd sell herself, or her panic at how close he'd come to the truth.

"My guess is blackmail. You're too naïve to even know how to begin doing business with these sorts on your own initiative. They approached you. So, what do you have that they want?"

She stared up at him, her lips pressed together defiantly. He could ask the question until the cows came home, but she was *not* going to answer him.

He leaned forward. It was a subtle thing, but he invaded her personal space...and not in a nice way. It wasn't even remotely sexual in overtone. It was just intimidating.

"We're out here all alone," he murmured in a silky tone. "You and me. Nobody for miles to hear you shout for help. I'm all you've got."

He said the words in threat, but they resonated all the way to her soul. *I'm all you've got.* Good Lord, he was exactly right. She had nobody else. Her parents, whom she might have turned to in a crisis, were at the heart of this one. Her younger brother, Mike, was flighty at best, and foolish at worst. Definitely not any help. Her colleagues, neighbors—she'd never bothered to get close to any of them, so involved in her work had she been over the years.

And men? People thought she had it easy in that department because she was reasonably good-looking. But they didn't realize that it got really annoying having to constantly fend off men on the prowl for easy sex with hot chicks. Somewhere along the way, she'd gotten so good at driving off the macho jerks that it had become a habit to push all men away.

She was headed down the fast track to withering up and becoming old and lonely before her time. Heck, she didn't even have anyone she'd call a friend. Oh, she had a few acquaintances whom she went out with socially now and then, but no one she'd tell her deepest, darkest secrets to.

She looked up at John in dismay. And was even more dismayed to realize her vision was strangely blurred and her eyes suddenly burned.

"Oh, for crying out loud," he muttered. "Do you have to go and get all weepy on me now?"

"Pardon me for having feelings," she sniffed. "We women happen to cry, occasionally, you know. Maybe you should give it a try, sometime."

He recoiled strongly from that suggestion. "No thanks," he shot back.

She frowned at the violence of his reaction. What was that all about? In a blatant attempt to deflect him from pursuing why she was crying, she announced, "You're so busy demanding to know everything about me and my life, but I don't see you telling me a whole hell of a lot about yourself."

"I'm the hired gun you bought to get you to your destination. I've played ball in this part of the world before. I know the players and I know the rules of the game. I can get you where you're going, and you're paying me top dollar to get you there in one piece. What more is there to know about me?"

She cast around for something personal to ask him. "What are you taking muscle relaxants for? And how did you get that gunshot wound in your back?"

He shoved away from the Land Rover and whirled away from her abruptly. Her eyebrows shot up as he presented her his back and shut her out in no uncertain terms. Uh-huh. That was what she thought. He was all hot and bothered to know her secrets, but he wasn't about to share any of his with her. It was okay for him to act all dark and tortured and mysterious, but it wasn't okay for her to be the same way.

He paced a few yards away and then spun and stalked back to her. She held her ground but not for lack of an urge to flee in the face of his advance.

"I hurt my back a few months ago. And to anticipate your next question, no, I'm not telling you how I got shot. So don't ask."

She reared back from the vehemence in his voice. Wow. She must have really hit a nerve. She asked casually, "How's your back feeling now? Are you up for a hike through the high Andes?"

"My back doesn't feel great, actually. It could have done without all that banging around in the Land Rover."

"Can I take a look at it?" she asked gently.

"What? Are you a doctor or something?"

"Yeah, or something."

His head jerked up. "Come again?"

She winced. She didn't often admit her academic credentials to men. It always seemed to put them off. Apparently, intelligent, educated women put off the kinds of guys who were drawn to women who looked like her. The jerks. Praying under her breath that John didn't fall into that class of men, she answered reluctantly, "Dr. Melina Montez, at your service."

"What kind of doctor?" he bit out sharply.

"Medical. But I don't practice. I do medical research."

"For a pharmaceutical firm," he affirmed neutrally.

She nodded. He didn't sound tremendously put off by her education. Of course, the proof of the pudding would be if he tried to bed her again or not.

"Do you test medications?" he asked.

"I develop new ones, actually," she corrected cautiously.

"Do you mistreat monkeys and run torture labs for rats?"

She laughed. "No. I don't do any animal testing. I work

with lots of boring chemical compounds in test tubes and use the occasional petri dish or Bunsen burner."

He absorbed that with far more thoughtfulness than she would have wished for. At least he didn't look completely put off by her profession. But she got the distinct impression he was making leaps of logic she could seriously do without him making just now. Did he always look for the angle behind what people said, the words unspoken? He certainly seemed to do it to her.

"Turn around," she directed in her best doctor voice. "Let me see your back."

He cocked an amused eyebrow at her. "You want me to take my shirt off?"

She pursed her lips. "You'd better not. It's going to be distracting enough having to put my hands on you."

He laughed quietly, a masculine sound of satisfaction.

Jerk, she thought without any real heat. She stepped up to him as he turned away from her. Even through the soft cambric of his shirt, his body heat scalded her palms as she laid them on his back. "Tell me where it hurts," she murmured.

"My lumbar vertebrae."

She nodded and slid her hands down heavy ridges of muscle to the small of his back. She expected to feel knots and corded muscles, but was surprised to feel smooth, supple tissue beneath her hands. "Any spinal injury?" she asked.

"MRIs showed hot spots on the L-3 and L-4 vertebrae where the bullet obliquely creased them."

He'd been lucky, then. If a bullet had lodged in that part of his spine, he'd be paralyzed from the waist down right now. The potential tragedy of that was doubly poignant to her after having made love with him and felt all his vital power from the waist down. "How long ago were you shot?"

He recited emotionlessly, "Eight months ago."

She frowned. That was plenty of time for the body to have

laid in calcium deposits and strengthened the affected area. He shouldn't still be in acute pain. But those painkillers back in the hotel said it all. "Did you lay off and rehab your back or did you keep pounding it after the initial injury?"

He was silent for a long time, as if reluctant to answer the question. Why? It wasn't a hard one.

Finally, he exhaled slowly. "I walked and crawled on it for thirty miles right after I was shot. The bullet wasn't removed for several days and it was pretty infected by the time a doctor saw it. I couldn't really clean it out myself. It took some extra time to heal."

Holy crap. Thirty miles? Shot in the back? Was that how far he'd been from a phone or help of any kind? Frankly, he was lucky to be alive. Bullet wounds were among the dirtiest of injuries. Not only was there the contamination from the lead, but then there was gunpowder, grease residue, dirt in an open wound and the deep, puncture nature of most bullet wounds to contend with. No bullet wound was supposed to go for *days* without treatment.

"Where in the world were you that it took so long to get medical care?"

"Just this side of hell."

Hmm. That was certainly an evasive answer. But the shadows in his eyes were much more informative. She would bet the farm that the circumstances of his getting shot were floating through his mind and putting that grim line of white around his mouth. In an effort to get him to talk some more, or at least to lighten his mood, she asked, "How'd the other guy fare?"

John all but collapsed in front of her. The strong, competent, in-control man before her crumpled in on himself, crossing his arms over his chest in what almost looked like a hug of agony. What on God's green earth could cause a man like John Hollister this much pain? Had he killed someone? If he had, she'd also bet it had been a bad guy, or had been an accident. He was far too honorable, too decent a man to have shot down anyone in cold blood with or without damned good reason.

"Talk to me, John. What happened? You can tell me. I'm a doctor. I'll treat it with patient confidentiality if you need me to."

The muscles beneath her hands turned to bands of tempered steel all of a sudden. He jerked away from her, spinning to face her. Whoa. Abruptly, his grief transformed into something dangerous. Dark. Lethal. He stared down at her with the blank, cold eyes of a killer. She recoiled sharply. Who was this man? He bore no resemblance whatsoever to the man who'd laughed and made love with her so recently. This man was terrifying.

"Don't ask me that again," he answered from between gritted teeth.

Frightened, she nodded up at him. Surely the man she knew and lusted after was in there somewhere. But he was buried very deep at the moment.

Apparently, he realized how badly he'd scared her, for he made a concerted effort to lower his shoulders. He even attempted a smile for her. He failed, and only produced a brief grimace, but it signaled the return of the moderately sane man behind the killer.

Her fear subsided somewhat, but she continued to eye him cautiously.

He ground out, "Thanks for your concern, Doc. But I've got it handled."

Right. And she was the Easter bunny. He stepped away from her and headed around the front of the Land Rover.

"Get in," he ordered from the other side of the vehicle.

Thoughtfully, she did as he said. He started the engine and pulled away grimly into the night.

Chapter 6

John didn't know what time it was when he finally pulled off the dirt road and hid the Land Rover behind a thick clump of bushes and vines. Melina disappeared into the darkness to relieve herself with strict orders not to go far. Meanwhile, he pulled armfuls of the vines across the top of the Land Rover, further disguising its presence. When he was satisfied that even a thorough look at this spot wouldn't reveal the vehicle, he moved their gear up to the front passenger seat, folded down the rear seats, and made a makeshift bed for them out of a couple blankets and her soft-sided suitcase full of clothes for a pillow.

He'd slept in worse. A personal favorite was the op he'd led in a Turkish sewer—running with raw sewage. It had taken him a month to get rid of the stink and longer to get the taste of that mission out of his mouth. But they'd gotten the kill, and one less psychopath was loose upon the world. And not one of his guys had complained about the conditions. It was the only approach to the target, so they'd sucked it up and gotten the job done. Good men. Dead men…

"Whatchya lookin' at?"

He jumped violently at Melina's cheerful voice behind him.

"Easy, Cowboy," she murmured. "It's just me."

Afraid she'd do that disconcerting thing again where she looked into his soul and stripped him bare, he mumbled, "Which half of the bed do you want?"

"As in left/right or top/bottom?"

His gaze snapped to her in surprise. He commented cautiously, "Most women find a good car chase and getting shot at too scary to be turned on by it."

She shrugged. "Life's short. Why waste a little privacy and a hot guy?"

He didn't know whether to laugh at her forwardness or be depressed that he was only some convenient stud for her. Faintly alarmed that he actually gave a damn what she thought of him, he settled for arching an eyebrow. "Hot, huh?"

She flashed a coquettish dimple. "Want me to show you how hot?"

The laugh won out and he chuckled. "Naughty *and* she likes to play doctor. You're some woman." The kind of woman who could make an honest man out of him. In different circumstances, of course. Another time and place, before his life went to hell and he forgot to die before he went there.

She tossed her head, sending her honey hair bouncing around her shoulders. "That's what they all say."

The undertone of dishonesty in her voice caught his attention. Not a lot of men in her life, huh? A surge of possessive pleasure startled him. He might not be able to keep her for the long term, but for the moment, she was his. And because that seemed like enough for her, he wasn't going to feel too guilty about taking advantage of her.

He took a step forward and laid his hands on her slender

waist. His fingers didn't quite span it, but he didn't fail by much. "You don't have much to do with men, do you?"

She blinked up at him in surprise. "Why do you say that?"

He gazed down at her, the thick blanket of night wrapping around them, hiding them from the rest of the world. "You're not jaded enough. Which probably means you haven't made the rounds of the dating scene a whole lot." But then he cocked his head, studying her further. "Or maybe it's that you're so jaded you've checked out on romance completely. Us guys do a number on beautiful women like you. Mess with your heads. By the time you've been dating for a few years, you start to get cynical. You swear off men for the most part. Which camp do you fall into?"

Momentary surprise flickered across her face. *Uh-huh. He'd gotten it right on the second guess.* She was one of those women whom men wouldn't leave alone. He murmured almost to himself, "But I think there may still be hope for you."

"What in the world makes you think that?" she asked, far too casually.

So, she'd declared herself lost long ago, had she? "You looked into my eyes last night. And you let me look into yours. That's a dangerous thing."

"Dangerous?"

He shrugged. "It takes guts to let someone look into your soul."

"You looked into my soul?" she asked, in what sounded suspiciously like dismay. "What did you see?"

"Honestly?"

She nodded up at him, her eyes dark and shuttered. Was she aware that her fingers were twisted in the front of his shirt, clutching almost violently at the cotton fabric? He reached up to save his shirt from a premature shredding, gently disentangling her fingers. "You can turn my shirt loose now."

"You're stalling," she accused. "What did you see?"

He sighed. "Probably the same thing you saw in my eyes."

"Which was?"

"Nothing. Nothing at all."

She went still all over, absorbing that with a pained intensity that surprised even him—and he'd been expecting her not to like his observation. She spun away, staring out into the night, which was to say, she was looking at nothing. It was damned dark out here, and there wasn't anything to see in this gloom anyway but a bunch of rocks and scrawny trees.

He opened the Land Rover's rear hatch and said, "Climb in. We both could use some rest."

"You're not going to insist on one of us standing guard while the other one sleeps?" she asked in surprise.

"I'm a light sleeper." Usually. Too bad he hadn't been sleeping light the night of the ambush. Maybe a few more of his men would still be alive today if he'd heard the Taliban patrol sneak up on their position. Hell, maybe they'd all be alive. Sure, there'd been other guys standing guard. But he was the commander. Ultimately responsible for all their lives. And he'd been asleep on the job. Hell, unconscious on the job.

He blinked away the nightmare swimming before his eyes yet again, and instead of seeing his men's bloody corpses, he was suddenly staring at a denim-cupped, juicy tush that would make any grown man sweat. He silently cursed himself as Melina crawled into the back of the Land Rover. He didn't deserve even one second's pleasure in this life while his men lay six feet under.

She took the passenger's side of the back, and he took the driver's side. They tossed and turned until they finally settled into positions of rough comfort. He propped his head and shoulders on her suitcase, and she curled up against his side, tucked under his outstretched arm, her head resting on his shoulder, her knee nestled far too comfortably against his groin. His bent knees flopped against the tire housing and the ribs of the truck bed only mildly dug into his back.

Damn, he could really use a pile of sleeping pills right about now.

And as soon as the thought entered his mind, there was no dislodging it. He couldn't think about anything but the sweet relief of chemically induced nothingness coursing through his veins, wiping away everything in its path. *Blessed oblivion, come to Papa....*

Except a freaking doctor was lying on top of his arm, effectively trapping him in more than one way. Who'd have guessed the hot chick in a short skirt who'd sashayed into Pirate Pete's was an M.D.? He swore under his breath at his rotten luck.

"John?"

"Hmm?"

"Are you scared?"

Hell yes, he was scared! Scared he couldn't make it through the night without his pills, scared he'd get another nightmare and wake up screaming or worse, crying like a baby. The shrinks said the nightmares would go away with time, but it had been months, and they were as vivid as ever, dammit. He really didn't need to embarrass himself in front of Melina.

Lying his ass off, he answered, "Nah, nothing scares me. Why? Are you?"

A small nod against his shoulder.

"Why?" He asked as gently as he could, infusing that simple question with as little interest as he could muster. Didn't want to scare her off completely of talking to him. And after his nearly violent outburst with her earlier, he'd better soft-shoe around her for a while. He'd seen the stark terror in her eyes when she looked at him, and it hadn't been pretty. He cursed himself yet again for putting that look in her eyes. He hurt everyone who got near him, dammit. He had no intention of killing her, too.

"I like being alive," she murmured.

The words shot through like an electric shock. His men had liked being alive, too. Yet he'd gotten them all killed.

As misery washed over him, drowning him in its icy depths, she added in a whisper that he thought maybe he hadn't been supposed to hear, "I don't want to die."

"Must be nice." He jolted to realize he'd made that comment aloud.

"I beg your pardon?"

"Never mind," he replied hastily. He had no intention of explaining that being alive held no great appeal to him, personally. He might have promised Brady Hathaway that he wouldn't kill himself until Mel was safely delivered to her final destination. But after that, he was checking out with all due haste. And that was that.

Melina could have all that perky, zest-for-living crap. But it did beg the question of why she'd made the comment. Why was she thinking about death? And why was she expressing her fear of it in terms that led him to believe she expected to die—and soon?

She snuggled in a little closer, her left hand roaming across his belly to lodge somewhere in the vicinity of his lower right rib cage. He'd get her to talk eventually. Her naturally honest and outgoing nature would betray her. She would either come to trust him enough, or he'd simply take advantage of a gregarious moment to get the truth out of her.

She was a hell of a woman. If he'd been planning to stay alive, he'd have to give serious consideration to giving up his career for her. He'd never been married—he was the kind of guy who didn't do anything halfway, and he'd never figured out how to have as demanding and capricious a career as the Special Forces and still manage to do a marriage justice. But nobody stayed in his business forever. The ones lucky enough to live eventually got out of the service and settled down to something approximating normalcy…assuming they could tame their demons enough to sleep at night.

He'd decided long ago that the woman didn't exist for whom he'd actually consider getting out of the business. But he hadn't met Melina Montez when he'd made that decision. She was something special, no doubt about it.

Her fingernails scraped lightly across his side, and he sucked in his breath, startled into momentary ticklishness.

"The big bad commando is ticklish?" she laughed.

"Commandos are human, too, you know," he retorted. "We have families and live normal lives and coach Little League and mow the lawn." Not that he'd ever gone for that, but several of his guys had—very successfully and happily. Until he'd gone and gotten them killed.

He shoved away recollection of those agonizing marches up front sidewalks to tell Judy Gill and Samantha Criswell and Marley Ledbetter that their husbands were coming home—but in flag-draped caskets. It had been the hardest thing he'd ever done to hand that folded flag to Bobby Criswell, who'd been all of nine years old and trying so damned hard not to cry at his daddy's funeral.

He swore violently under his breath. He needed something. Now. He didn't care if it was carisoprodol or a bottle of vodka or a sledgehammer between the eyes...something, anything to take away the pain!

He shifted restlessly. Abruptly, the back of the Land Rover felt suffocatingly small, its sides closing in on him inch by inch.

"Are you okay?" Melina murmured.

"Yeah, I'm fine. I'm just longer than the backseat of a Land Rover."

"Do you want to shift more diagonally so you can stretch your legs out?"

"No, I'm fine. I'm sorry to disturb you. Go to sleep." He managed not to snap at her…he thought.

She pulled back from him like she was offended. What was wrong with her? A cool hand touched his forehead and he jumped, startled.

"You're sweating," she announced.

"Thanks for that update, Doc."

She sat up at that. "Give me your wrist. I want to take your pulse."

"I thought you said you don't practice medicine."

"That doesn't mean I don't know how to do it."

"Lie down. I'll be okay. It was just a rough day."

"No, it wasn't. Not for you. It was a hell of a day for me, but you were as cool as a cucumber the whole time. You didn't show the slightest sign of stress until about two minutes ago."

"Delayed reaction," he ground out.

"Not buying it," she announced blithely. "Gimme your wrist."

She was one of those women you just knew would get more stubborn the more you dug in your heels with her. Rather than argue all damned night about her taking his pulse, he handed over his wrist and pressed his lips together in irritation. "I suppose you have a blood pressure cuff and a stethoscope in your bag, too."

"Be quiet," she ordered.

He rolled his eyes while she counted his pulse for the next week-and-a-half. Finally, she let his wrist go.

"I don't need a blood pressure cuff or a stethoscope. I've had my ear on your chest for the past five minutes, and I heard your heart beating harder and faster the longer I lay there."

Damn. He bluffed with desperate aplomb, "What can I say? You have that effect on me."

"Mmm. I like the sound of that. Too bad it's a lie."

He stared up at her in the dark. He was an accomplished liar. He was professionally trained to be good at it! And she'd seen through him like he was a freshly washed window.

He didn't know what to say next. All the usual putoffs he gave doctors—she'd brushed past them like they were pesky gnats. He had no more gambits left. There was always the truth, of course. But if he'd managed for eight months not to spill his guts to shrinks who extracted confessions from special operators for a living, there was no way he was telling this woman after knowing her for two days. She already was looking at him weirdly and he needed her to follow his instructions without hesitation if things got dicey for them again. He didn't need her thinking he was a complete nutcase and questioning everything he told her to do.

He could make it through the night. Just one night without the sleeping pills. No big deal. He had superhuman self-discipline. Could tolerate vast amounts of fatigue. Had pain tolerances that most people couldn't even imagine, let alone achieve. He could lie here and grit his teeth for six hours if he had to, no matter how jumpy and desperate he felt.

Thankfully, she lay back down beside him.

"Could you relax your shoulder muscles a little, John? They're as hard as steel right now and frankly don't make a very comfortable headrest."

"Take the duffel bag. It's full of clothes."

"No, that's okay. I like your shoulder. Just less tense."

He did his best to relax. He really did. He went through all the usual exercises, releasing his muscles one by one, working his way down from his forehead to his toes. But by the time he got to his knees each time, the back of his shoulders were knotted up as badly as ever.

Melina finally sat up again. "Roll over on your stomach."

"Huh?"

"Roll over. I'm giving you a back rub."

"I don't need one. Really."

She merely knelt, glaring down at him in expectant silence. Damn, that woman was pushy!

He huffed and levered himself over onto his belly, his legs bent at the knees and his heels sticking up in the air. Not exactly dignified, but he forgot all about it when Mel swung her left thigh over his upper legs, straddling him between her soft inner thighs. *Hell-o.*

Her hands were heaven. She wasn't afraid to use some force to really knead into the muscles. The pleasure bordered on pain, and couldn't have been more perfect. *Add Swedish-caliber masseuse to her long list of assets.*

"You keep popping up with talents like this and I'm gonna have to marry you," he groaned.

Her hands went still on his back. "I beg your pardon?"

He frowned, trying to recapture what he'd just said. Talents…marriage…*oh, crap*. He tried to sit up, but she was planted squarely on his buttocks at the moment, and unless he threw her against the roof, she wasn't budging.

"I'm sorry," he said quickly. "I didn't mean anything by that. I was just talking smack. You give a hell of a back rub, Mel."

Her hands went back to kneading below his left shoulder blade. "Thanks. You just startled me. I don't think of myself in terms of being marriage material."

He tried to look over his shoulder and only ended up hurting his neck. "Why the hell not? What man wouldn't want you? Surely you have to fight guys off with a stick."

"Not so much anymore."

He snorted. "Is that pharmaceutical firm you work at a nunnery or something?"

She laughed. "Hardly. More like a shark farm."

"Ahh. The men come on too strong?"

He felt her shrug through her palms. "They're mostly traditional Hispanic men. I'm an empowered American woman who happens to want something more than being barefoot and pregnant in the kitchen. We don't always see eye-to-eye on how a relationship should go."

He grinned against his forearm. He'd bet not.

"Roll over," she ordered. She lifted up, partially off of him, but it was clear that she intended to continue her attentions on his front side—still straddling his hips.

His breath caught in his throat. Okay, then. Give the good doctor high marks for distracting him from little plastic bottles of pills. He complied, rolling onto his back awkwardly. His shoulder blades had barely touched the truck bed before her mouth was on his, her breasts mashing against his through their shirts.

"Touching you like that turns me on," she mumbled against his mouth. "I hope you don't mind."

He laughed in actual, physical pain—but not in his back—his reaction to her was so fast and hard. "Touch me some more," he mumbled back.

They banged their knees and elbows and got tangled up in shirtsleeves and shoelaces, and ended up laughing in each other's arms, finally mostly naked. He reached up to cup her breasts, to test their weight and resilience, and she arched her back, throwing her head back on a gasp of pleasure. Man. Talk about responsive. He was willing to go slow, to pleasure her the way she'd already pleasured him by putting her hands all over him. But she was having none of it. Her hair swung forward in a curtain around her face as she fumbled between them, and then she was sliding down over him, all slick heat, a tight glove of exquisite sensation that made his buttocks clench harder than steel beneath her.

She gave a patented Melina hip rock and groaned. He matched the sound, then gritted out between clenched teeth, "Do that again."

She complied. And shuddered around him. He gaped up at her. She was there already? Ho-ly cow. He moved beneath her, and she moaned again. She matched his motion, and they quickly found a rhythm between them.

A loud squeak sounded and Melina froze above him. "What was that?"

He grinned widely. "That, darlin', was the Land Rover's shock absorbers. We're giving this poor old bucket a worse workout than it got in those gullies."

She giggled, collapsing on his chest in embarrassment and humor. "I've never done it in a car," she confessed.

He shook his head in mock horror. "What was wrong with the boys in your high school? How could they let down the male half of the species like that?"

She sat up once more. "Look! The windows are fogged over and everything!"

He laughed up at her. "Next time we'll do it in the front seat. You haven't lived until you've had sex with a gearshift jabbing you in the side. Everyone should experience it at least once before they die."

It was as if an arctic wind blew through the air. She froze, and all the joy drained out of her like water pouring from a glass.

"What's wrong, Mel? Talk to me, sweetheart."

She shook her head violently and her hair spilled down around her face, a veil he couldn't see past. He reached up to push it back, to look into her eyes, but she moved determinedly, riding him hard and fast with a desperation that bordered on manic. He wanted to stop. To ask her what in the hell had just happened. But the demands of her body pulling at his, sliding up and down his shaft like a jackhammer, battering against him as if the world were about to end, were too much.

He closed his eyes and allowed her to suck him into the moment, to wipe all thought from his mind, to fill him with a lust so bright and pure and hot it seared away everything but sheer sensation. The world narrowed down to her perspiration-slicked body slamming against his, his equally galvanized body shivering beneath hers, arching up, meeting her thrusts with his own, driving into her with every ounce of his strength.

And then the orgasm started, shimmering outward in ever-expanding circles until it consumed his entire being, building into an explosion that convulsed his entire body into a single giant spasm of release, a shout tearing from his throat at the same moment she keened a long, waivering note of her own release.

He shuddered once. Twice. A third time. And finally, finally, the orgasm released its hold on him. He collapsed back against the hard, cold floor, wrung out to the dregs of his existence. Melina collapsed on his chest, breathing like a spent racehorse. He knew the feeling. Sweat lubricated their entire bodies and she slid easily against him when, a few minutes later, she finally pressed up onto her elbows to stare down at him.

He did push her hair back then, determined to see what was in her oh-so-expressive gaze. She might lie to him with her mouth, but her eyes had never lied to him. She didn't resist this time when he split the curtain of golden silk and tucked her hair behind her neck, holding it there lightly. He stared up at her, and she stared back at him in the darkness.

And what he saw in her unwillingly, painfully honest gaze made his blood run cold.

It wasn't fear.

Or desperation.

Or even despair.

It was nothing. Absolutely nothing at all.

It might as well have been a mirror into his own soul, for he was staring into the abyss.

Chapter 7

By the time they caught sight of a village late the next morning, Melina felt like a giant bruise from head to foot from sitting in the car so long. Silently, they drove along the floor of a deep valley between towering twin peaks. There'd been utter silence between them since that devastating moment last night when John gazed into the depth of her soul, and finally recoiled from what he saw.

Not that she blamed him. She'd come out here to die, plain and simple, and he'd seen it clear as day in her gaze. Thankfully, he hadn't belabored the point with pleas to reconsider or lectures about the preciousness of life. She knew all that. Heck, she didn't *want* to die. But the situation was what it was. And she had no more choices left.

She started when John actually broke the silence, speaking emotionlessly. "That's where we're going."

She looked up at the line of peaks soaring at least a thousand feet above them and gulped. This was the place where she was supposed to rendezvous with Huayar's men and get further instructions. A long series of switchbacks led from the valley floor up one of the mountains to a village perched at its summit. There it was. The point of no return.

She ventured a glance over at John. As it had been since they made love last night, his jaw was set in lines of stone, and his eyes were...dead.

Under normal circumstances it would have scared the hell out of her. But as it was, she knew exactly how he felt. She didn't know why he felt that way, but she recognized the great void of black despair yawning inside him the same way it did inside of her.

With every mile behind them, the darkness consumed a little more of her. In another few minutes, John would hand her over to Huayar's men and leave her. The oppressive weight of her looming fate made breathing difficult. John would say it was just the altitude getting to her, but she knew better. She would be well and truly lost.

John guided the Land Rover around the first switchback.

She knew the source of her despair. It had come upon her the moment she'd made her decision. When the ransom letter arrived from Huayar demanding that she hand herself over to him in return for the lives of her brother Mike, and her parents, it had taken her about thirty seconds to absorb the implications of her choice and about another two seconds to decide that she was willing to sacrifice herself to save her family.

John downshifted and went around another switchback.

Nope, not a difficult decision at all. Just an incredibly painful one. Thing was, she liked living. Not that her life was any great shakes. She spent most of her waking hours locked in her lab, experimenting with common over-the-counter chemicals, trying to find a formula to replace methamphetamine as the next designer drug of the new millennium. Not with the intent to market it, of course, but rather to help governments and pharmaceutical firms anticipate which common chemicals and medications needed to be regulated and controlled. And if she was lucky, to find a way to counteract its negative effects.

Still, she enjoyed the little things in life—sunlight on her face. The feel of the ocean on her feet. The song sparrow who serenaded her faithfully every morning outside her bedroom window. Old movies and pizza with double pepperoni and pajamas warm out of the dryer.

Another switchback.

The choice was simple. Her life or the lives of the three people she loved most in the world. It was no choice at all. And in the moment when she'd come to understand that, darkness had claimed her soul.

The Land Rover groaned a little as the road grew steeper and spiraled around another hairpin curve. John downshifted again.

She didn't want to die, dammit!

And then there was John himself. In his arms she'd found a joy she'd never dreamed existed, let alone was possible for her. He made love to her with his entire being, like she was the only other person on Earth. It was extraordinary. It completely consumed her, and she thought maybe he felt the same way. And for just an instant—long enough to remember what it felt like to breathe—making love with him held back the darkness.

"Stop the car, John," she said abruptly.

He did so with alacrity. "What's up?"

"I need you to promise me something."

"What?" In a single word, his curiosity was replaced by caution.

"Please don't mess this up for me. I'm making a deal with these guys, and at all costs, I need that deal to happen. No matter what you think of it, you have to promise not to interfere or screw it up."

That sent both of his eyebrows sailing upward. But then that mask of his that showed absolutely nothing of his thoughts settled back into place. "And if I don't promise?"

"Then I'm firing you, getting out of this car, and walking the rest of the way up the mountain by myself. I *am* going to go through with this deal."

He nodded grimly to himself as if in confirmation. "It is blackmail, then. What do you have to sell, and what are they offering you?"

Her lips thinned into a tight, white line.

He threw up a hand in surrender. "All right. Fine. Don't tell me. I'm your greatest asset, but if you refuse to take advantage of what I can do for you, there's nothing I can do about it. I promise not to block your deal."

"You swear?" she asked nervously.

His brows slammed down hard. "Honey, I may not be a lot of things, but I am a man of my word. If I say I will or won't do something, you can bet your life on it."

And that was exactly what she was doing. She was betting her life and her family's life on him keeping his word. It had been a huge risk to bring anyone along with her on this journey at all, let alone a big, strong, capable guy like him. She could only pray his presence didn't tick off Huayar so badly that the crime lord backed out of the deal. But she'd simply been too scared—too weak—to do this by herself.

"Are we ready to proceed?" John asked tersely. "The lookouts are no doubt beginning to wonder what the hell we're doing, just sitting here like this. And believe me, you don't want to make these guys suspicious. They'll shoot first and ask questions later."

"How do you know who these people are?" she shot back.

This time a single eyebrow arched sardonically. "I already told you. I've run around in this part of the world before. I know where I am, and I know whose turf I'm operating on."

She sighed. He was entirely too smart for his own good. Thank goodness he'd promised to behave himself. "Let's go."

His jaw muscles rippling, he threw the Land Rover into gear and it lurched into motion.

Here went nothing.

The village looked much like the last one, except the houses clung precariously to the side of the mountain in terraced rows with narrow, stone streets between them. It was dusty and poor and strangely devoid of pedestrians, just like the last village.

"Where is everybody?" she murmured.

"Hiding. When a stranger comes to town, they don't want to get caught in the cross fire."

"You make it sound like gunslingers duel in the streets around here."

"They do."

"But…that's barbaric!"

He asked sharply, "Where did you get the crazy idea that this was a civilized corner of the world?"

"Point taken. Thank goodness I brought along a hired gun of my own, eh?" She was trying to lighten the mood, but his grim nod of agreement wrecked the attempt.

"I tremble to think what would happen to you if I weren't here," he grumbled under his breath.

She reached across the vehicle to squeeze his knee in gratitude. "I'm glad you're here, too, John. I couldn't do this without you."

"Whatever the hell *this* is," he muttered to himself.

She gazed apprehensively out the window at the gray stone buildings, the same color as the mountain from whence they came. The day was cloudy, with a cool haze hanging below a low ceiling of clouds. It fit her mood.

"Here we are," John announced in a brisk, businesslike tone.

She stared at the nondescript building before her. Two stories tall, it looked exactly the same as every other building on the street, except for a small, rusted plaque beside the door. The word Cantina was more missing than present. What letters weren't rusted out appeared to have been shot out. Not an encouraging sign. She jumped when her car door opened. John had come around to her side of the vehicle to open it and she'd been too distracted to notice. She had to get her head in the game. Fast.

"Don't hesitate," he murmured. "We're being watched."

She nodded and climbed out. She turned to face the pub, and was immensely relieved when John's hand came to rest in the small of her back. She resisted an urge to turn into him, to burrow against his chest and hide in his strong arms. Strong. She had to be strong for Mike and for her parents.

He ushered her to the door and pushed it open before her. She was surprised when he stepped inside in front of her, effectively blocking her passage. He paused for several long seconds. It dawned on her belatedly that he was checking the place out before he let her go inside. Yup. A hired gun of her own.

He stepped aside, and she eased inside, trying not to convey exactly how terrified she was by her expression or movement. This time John merely touched her elbow, guiding her across the room to a table in the far corner. He conspicuously took the seat that put his back against two walls.

"Sit beside me on my left," he instructed quietly.

She nodded and did as he said. A small man who looked like a sun-dried raisin came over to their table and asked cautiously if they would like something to drink. John replied easily that the two of them would both like something nonalcoholic and in a can—unopened.

A significant look passed between him and the bartender. The two men nodded slightly, as if they'd just had an entire conversation that she'd missed. As the man went away to get their drinks, she leaned toward John and breathed, "What was that all about?"

A supremely unconcerned expression on his face, he

replied under his breath, "No one can slip anything in our drink if it comes out of a pressurized, unopened can. I just served notice to the locals that I'm no amateur, and they will have to go through me to get to you."

"You promised you wouldn't—"

He cut her off quickly. "And I won't. But there are going to be a few ground rules, for your safety and mine. I'm just establishing those up front."

She only vaguely understood what he was talking about. It all sounded like testosterone-induced posturing to her. The thing about the tampered drinks made sense, though. She had to give him credit for that. She wouldn't have thought of it herself.

The raisin guy set two sodas, still in the can and unopened, on the table in front of them. John smiled and peeled off a nice-size bill from his money clip and passed it to the guy with a word of thanks and directions to keep the change. The guy's eyes lit up and he smiled a little more widely at them.

"Hmm. Interesting," John murmured.

"How so?"

"The bartender is a low-level flunky. That measly tip was significant to him, which means he's not paid a lot by the big boys, hence he's not far up the food chain. This may take a while."

"Why?"

"We'll have to work our way up through layers of management, as it were, to get to the folks you're really here to talk to. Get ready to do a whole lot of soda drinking, babe."

His prediction wasn't wrong. Over the course of the next several hours, a half-dozen men wandered into the joint and made their way to the table in the back corner. John made it crystal clear that it was her job to sit there and sip sodas while he did all the early-round talking. And she had to admit, he was really good at it. He was pleasant and relaxed with everyone, and he put all the interviewers at ease. He never hinted at anything threatening or did any macho posturing. He was respectful and quiet, and the locals seemed impressed with him. Lord knew she was, too. No way would her patience have held up like this. She'd have been ranting and raving and demanding to see Huayar in person hours ago.

"Ahh. Now we're getting somewhere," John muttered as the cantina door opened once more and the red light of sunset streamed inside the bar. The joint's true dinginess shone in stark relief for a moment, and then the door swung closed once more, cloaking the establishment in more flattering half-light.

She gazed at the pair of men who'd walked into the bar. One of them was noticeably better dressed than the other locals, his long-sleeved white shirt pressed, starched and well-tailored. His jeans weren't threadbare, and his boots were made of ostrich skin. A definite step up the crime ladder.

John gestured easily to the seats across from them. "May I buy you a drink, gentlemen?"

The new men nodded and ordered a local brand of beer she'd never heard of. Only when the brown bottles had been delivered and the bartender had retreated, did the crisply dressed one speak. "Miss Montez, we've been awaiting your arrival. What delayed you?"

She started at being addressed directly. She glanced over at John to see if he wanted to intervene, but he merely shrugged slightly and indicated that she should answer. "Uhh, there was no delay. It took a few days to get the right travel papers to come down here. I'm sorry if I worried you."

Something nudged her foot warningly—from John's side of the table. He must not want her apologizing to these guys. She supposed it did show weakness. And one must never show weakness to jackals if one didn't want to be said jackals' next meal.

"Have you got what you said you would bring?"

"I keep my promises, Mr.—" She let the question hang in the air.

"Call me Fuego."

Fuego? Fire? A little heavy-handed on the machismo, but whatever. "I keep my promises, Mr. Fuego."

"Just Fuego, Miss Montez."

"As you wish. Tell me, Fuego, do you have what I want, as well?"

He shrugged and she pressed, "The deal is they will be safe and unharmed when they are returned to me. Your employer has kept his word, has he not? My family is all right, yes?"

She glanced out the corner of her eye and realized that John had gone stock-still in his seat. Shock was quickly being chased from his expression by something cold and dangerous—killing rage. Abject relief that she'd extracted her promise from him before they'd come in here flooded her. The next time she glanced over at him, his expression was completely bland, as casual as it had been all afternoon.

"We have done as we promised, Miss Montez. Your family is alive."

"And unhurt?" she pressed.

The guy looked irritated at the pressure. "They are fine," he finally conceded.

She leaned back in her seat, so relieved she felt ill. She wanted to ask what came next, to get this guy to spell out the details of the trade, but John would no doubt kick her under the table if she looked too eager. Besides, her throat was too tight to speak without choking, which would make her look weak and panicky. As hard as it was for her to rein in her impatience, she sat there, sipping at a tepid soda, and waited for Fuego to do something with the big, fat ball bouncing around in the middle of his court. The man stared at her for several long minutes. It felt like forever, but she managed not to squirm under his scrutiny.

Finally, the guy leaned forward. "My employer is eager to speak with you."

"And I with him. I want to get this over with as soon as possible."

"Unfortunately, he is not here this week. He is…on a retreat…in the mountains. You may wait here for him, or you may go to him if you are in a hurry."

John leaned forward. "How far up into the mountains is this retreat?"

Fuego glanced over at him in irritation, like John was an impudent underling who didn't know his proper place. It amused her to think that Fuego might have underestimated her gunslinger. But then, maybe that was the idea. She sat back and let John play his game. She watched as he threw a rather dull look at Fuego, the kind that hired muscle without a lot of brain cells to spare might use. It would have amused her if so damn much wasn't at stake.

"How far?" John repeated. "I ain't no fan of nature hikes in no jungle. Too many damned bugs and critters."

In fact, the high mountains of Peru were carpeted in arboreal rain forests, which were a far cry from the tropical jungle of the lower altitudes, but then she suspected John knew that.

Fuego shrugged. "It's a few days away. Not bad if you know what you're doing. But for you…" He let the insult hang in the air, unspoken.

John's eyes took on a truculent glint. "I didn't say I can't camp and hike. I just said I don't like it. I mean, who in hell wants to go anywhere without television and cold beer?"

She bit back a smile at that one.

Contempt glittered in Fuego's gaze. "If I give you a set of coordinates, do you think you could find them?"

John shrugged. "Sure thing."

Fuego pulled a ballpoint pen out of his coat pocket—sporting the logo of a Las Vegas casino—and scribbled on a water-ringed napkin. He pushed the scrawled string of numbers across the table at her. She looked down at them, barely able to read the messy scrawl.

"Three days. Be there by sunset, or they die."

And with that grim announcement, Fuego abruptly pushed back from the table and stood up. Melina started as John mirrored the movement. Fuego lurched in surprise as John's hand snaked out so fast the guy didn't even get a chance to flinch, and trapped the guy's neck in an iron grip.

"Give your boss a message for me, will ya, Foo-ay-go? No matter how long it takes us to hike up to him, he touches one hair on any of his hostages' heads before we get there, and he'll regret ever being born. You catch my drift? We'll get there when we get there, and he'll damned well be waiting for us with a smile on his face and her family happy, well fed, and without a scratch on 'em."

"Or else what?" Fuego hissed.

John let go of the guy's throat with a little shove. While the guy stumbled and righted himself, John settled into what could only be interpreted as a trained-fighting stance. When he didn't answer the thug's question, Melina glanced up at him. And gulped. There was one, and only one way to describe the look in his eyes. Death.

Fuego took a careful step backward. Another. Then he turned and sauntered out of the place with patently false bravado. It was obvious the guy's shoulder blades were itching like mad and he was restraining an impulse to jump and run.

The door closed behind Fuego and his henchman and everyone in the room audibly let out a collectively held breath.

"C'mon, Mel," John muttered. "Let's get out of here before Fuego and his pals get any bright ideas."

He dropped several large bills on the table and nodded at the bartender, who nodded back. John called out a polite thanks for the man's hospitality, and then he and Melinda stepped outside into the cool evening. John went first again, pausing in the door to take a good look around before he stepped fully outside. He didn't have to say a word to get her to hustle into the Land Rover.

John wasted no time starting the engine and heading down the narrow street. They departed town from the opposite way they'd entered. The road deteriorated fast as it wound even higher into the mountains, and the going was slow.

They'd been driving for maybe two hours in charged silence, and full night was upon them when he stopped the car abruptly. The terrain around them was rocky, and trees loomed overhead, intensifying the night's darkness.

John pivoted in his seat to face her. He exploded, "*They've got your family?* Why in *bloody hell* didn't you tell me that before?"

Chapter 8

Fury flowed through John, hot and bright, burning away the fog that had enveloped him for the past eight months. He hadn't even known it was there until Mel made him this mad and banished the blanket of numbness that had shrouded him. He almost felt…alive.

"Tell me everything," he enunciated carefully past the control he was barely exercising on his temper. "Right now. I want to know everything."

Melina had the good sense to look scared. "Don't you understand?" she cried softly. "This is my family we're talking about! I can't risk them by involving you any more!"

"You can and you will."

She shook her head in mute denial.

"Look. I can open that door, shove you out, and leave you in the middle of nowhere. Right here and right now. Give me one good reason why I should continue with this mission if you won't be honest with me."

Sorrowfully, she made eye contact with him. "Because you care about me…at least a little bit?" When he didn't reply, she added, "Didn't the past two nights mean anything to you at all?"

That was a low blow. But it wasn't like he didn't deserve it. He sighed as some of his fury drained from him. "Do you want to die?" he asked her wearily.

"Actually, I expect to before this is all said and done."

He stared at her, truly shocked. And after a decade in this business, he was a damned hard man to shock. "Come again?"

"You heard me," she snapped with a hint of her usual fire.

"Why do you expect to die?" he burst out. As screwed up as he was in the head, even he would never go into an op assuming he was going to die in it.

She sighed. "I got a phone call four days ago. The man said they had my brother and my parents and they would torture them and start sending me body parts if I didn't do exactly as they said."

John prompted, "And they said to tell no one else, particularly the police."

She nodded.

"Then what did you do?"

"I went to a clinic and got the shots I'd need to come to Peru, took vacation from work, told everyone a lie about needing to get away for a while, and then I headed for Pirate Pete's."

"Why did you come to Pete's? Did someone tell you about us?"

"My brother used you guys once to deliver a package for him. I remembered him saying that Pirate Pete's would take anything anywhere and not ask too many questions. And I knew I couldn't make this trip on my own." She laughed ruefully. "It's not like you can walk up to some stranger and say, 'Excuse me, would you mind taking me to the hideout of some violent criminal in Peru?'"

"So you knew you were leading me into a death trap."

She flinched at that one. "I hoped not."

He was probably within his rights to ream her out for dragging him blind into this, but he wasn't entirely sure he blamed her. If his family's lives had been on the line, he might've done the very same thing. Desperation was a funny thing. It made you do stuff you never dreamed you'd do under normal circumstances.

He never imagined he'd crawl away from the bloody corpses of his guys, but it had been that or die himself. Not that he'd been all that keen on surviving that black night. But somebody had to make it back to base, to tell the tale of his men's heroism, to muster a recovery op to bring back their bodies. It was one of the most sacred creeds of the Special Forces. They never left behind one of their own…alive or dead.

"Okay. So you came to Pirate Pete's and hired me to bring you down here. Did you have any communication with the kidnappers between the time you walked into the store, and when you and I left the island?"

"No."

"Are you sure?" he asked.

She frowned. "Yes, I'm sure. I swear, I'm telling you the truth."

"You were told to go to Lima and then call that phone number. Anything else?"

"Yeah. I was told to hurry if I didn't want to start receiving ears and fingers in the mail."

"Do you know who these people are?" It was the critical question. He could only hope that by getting her to open up about the other stuff, she'd tell him the truth on this one, now.

"I don't know," she replied.

"What language did the guy speak to you in?"

"Spanish."

"Native? Mexican Spanish? Castilian Spanish? Could you tell anything about where the speaker was from?"

She paused, thinking about it. "I'd guess some variant of South American Spanish. But then, we're in Peru, aren't we?"

"Yeah, last time I checked." He thought for a moment. "Did he say anything at all that might be construed as having political overtones? Mention of a cause? Any political words like rebels or revolution or even the word government?"

"Nothing. I don't think the kidnappers are political. Frankly, I'm convinced they're criminals."

He pounced on that. "Why?"

"Why else would they want me?"

His eyebrows shot up. Now they were getting somewhere. "Do tell," he commented blandly, doing his best to conceal his excitement.

"Well, think about what I do. I research synthetic drugs."

He frowned. "Aren't most drugs synthetic these days?"

"I don't develop medicine. I create bad drugs. As in synthetic heroin. Methamphetamines. Illegal drugs."

Holy crap. "And you're on the payroll of an international pharmaceutical firm!" he exclaimed.

She laughed. "It's not like that. They know what I'm doing."

"Huh?"

"When methamphetamine was invented, the ingredients to make it were readily available over the counter. It took governments and law enforcement years to catch up with regulating the ingredients. Rather than wait for the next designer drug to hit the streets and then try to regulate the chemicals to make it, we're taking a proactive approach this time. I work with commonly available substances in a laboratory and see if I can concoct compounds with hallucinatory or addictive qualities."

"And have you succeeded?"

"As a matter of fact, I have. The compound still isn't perfected, but I've hit upon the basic process for making what may very well turn out to be the next widely popular illegal drug of the twenty-first century."

Whoa. No wonder her family had been snatched. "How long has your discovery been public knowledge? Surely the Mexican authorities knew to provide your family with round-the-clock security. How much force was required to overpower their guards and kidnap them?"

His mind raced with the complications this posed. He could be up against a veritable army up here in the mountains! This twist made it more imperative than ever that he get some backup before he and Melina reached the kidnappers' hideout.

Melina frowned. "My work isn't public knowledge."

He snorted. "Somebody knows, honey, or we wouldn't be sitting out here having this conversation."

"It's not possible. I'm the only person allowed in or out of my lab. Most of the executives at the company have no idea what I do, other than the fact that the government pays all my expenses."

"Most of the executives?"

"I found the compound before Christmas. And no one kidnapped my family before now. Surely if there were going to be a leak, it—and any reaction to it—would have happened before this."

Christmas. Over five months ago. That was a long time for a reaction to a discovery of this magnitude, had word of it gotten out. "Does anyone else know?"

"Just my parents. But they'd never tell. They understand how dangerous it would be for me if anyone else were to know about my discovery."

"Your brother?" he asked.

She shook her head. "He can be…immature. I haven't mentioned it to him."

"What's his name?"

"Michael."

He pulled out his cell phone and speed dialed H.O.T. Watch

Ops. While he waited for it to connect, he noticed Melina staring at him like he'd grown horns. "What?" he muttered.

"There are no cell phone towers out here!"

He shrugged. "You're right. That's why I'm using a satellite phone."

A female voice said in his ear, "Go ahead, Cowboy."

"Hiya, Raven." Raven was the call sign of Jennifer Blackfoot, the commander of the civilian side of the house within H.O.T. Watch. She was an extremely sharp cookie.

"Is White Horse around?" That was his boss's, Brady Hathaway's, field handle.

"Nope. He'll be out for at least the next two weeks. A search-and-rescue in a remote location."

John swore under his breath. Search-and-rescue missions often turned into frustrating and fruitless searches for needles in haystacks. They could take weeks to complete or finally be called off. His boss was well and truly out of the picture for a good long time. John scowled. It wasn't that he objected in any way to working with Agent Blackfoot. But right now, he needed a Spec Ops team in the worst way. They'd spent the past year cross-training the military and civilian sides of the H.O.T. Watch house for just this sort of occasion. Apparently, he was the lucky bastard who got to put the training to the test.

He said, "Pirate Pete's delivered a package for a guy named Michael Montez a while back. I need to know what we've got on him and that delivery."

"We'll get right on it. Anything else?" Jennifer replied.

"Yeah. I've got a hostage situation on my hands. Three civilians. This Montez kid and my client's parents are being held by probable drug dealers operating out of this area. Standby for the coordinates we've been given for our next rendezvous."

Cool as a cucumber after she'd copied down the numbers, Jennifer asked, "Do you want us to run a profile on your client?"

A stab of regret pierced him. But there was no help for it. This was life and death stuff they were dealing with out here. There was no time for emotion or personal feelings. "Oh, yeah," he replied. He dared not take a chance that she was holding out on him any further. This op had gone from milk toast to high explosives in the blink of an eye.

"We're on it. What else do you need, Cowboy?"

"I need a team down here, ASAP. Covert insertion, area surveillance, regional intel, threat analysis. The works."

A pause. "Peru isn't a country I can randomly insert a full-blown team into without involving the powers that be. It's going to take a little time to arrange."

"The Tangos are threatening to torture and kill three American hostages, and I believe this bunch will do it. I can slowball our trek, but we've got three, maybe four days to pull this thing together."

"Understood. I'll do my best."

Her best was usually formidable. "Thanks, Raven."

"I'll call when we have a briefing package for you."

He disconnected the call. And looked up into a pair of snapping black eyes that would have struck him dead if they could. "What?" he asked Melina a bit irritably.

"You made my brother sound like a criminal!"

"No, I asked for more information on a possible connection to this mission."

"He's not connected to this! He's a prisoner, at risk of dying, for goodness' sake."

John shrugged. "He's a possible leak. My people are going to have a look at him."

"Who were you talking to, anyway?"

"Some friends. Back at Pirate Pete's."

"And you think a bunch of mail haulers and bush pilots can find out about some drug lord who's running around down here kidnapping folks?"

He shrugged. "You'd be surprised. It's all about who you know, and we have a few connections here and there. If someone owes us a favor, we can ask a question or two."

"If you drag your buddies into this, let the record show their lives are on your head, not mine."

Her words were a dagger straight to his gut. He gasped in physical pain and struggled to draw his next breath. She might as well have given him a sharp blow to his solar plexus. *His buddies' lives were on his head.* Christ. He couldn't go there again. How long he sat there, gasping like a fish out of water, he didn't know.

Finally, he gathered himself enough to say, "We've got to get well away from this car before daylight. Let's go."

"So you'll go with me?" she cried out joyfully.

"Are there any more bombshells you haven't dropped on me yet?" he retorted.

"No. That's everything."

He shook his head. "Then I guess I'm going with you. I can't let a lamb like you walk into a den of lions all by yourself."

She reached over and squeezed his hand. Her touch shot through him like a hot shower on a cold day. That woman sure had gotten under his skin.

To her credit, Melina held up fairly well through the initial trek away from the Land Rover. She must work out in her spare time. That, and having lived in Mexico City at five-thousand-foot altitude, their current altitude of around nine thousand feet hadn't done her in completely.

But even he was feeling the thin air, complete with a distinctive altitude headache and lightheadedness, by the time dawn began to tint the sky in front of them. He paused, and Mel pulled up beside him and sank to the ground gratefully, panting.

"What do you say we find a nice hidey-hole and get some rest?" he said.

"I thought you'd never ask."

"You should've said something if you needed to stop. I'm not out here to kill you, Mel."

He winced at the pained look that flashed across her face. Okay, poor choice of words. "You sit there and rest. I'll build us a shelter."

She nodded wearily as he moved off, looking for a likely spot. He found a pair of fallen trees lying side by side about six feet apart. It would be a tight squeeze for the two of them, but for camouflage, he couldn't ask for better. Efficiently, he slung a tarp between the logs, being careful not to disturb the layers of moss on the bark as he lashed the roof into place. A couple minutes of tossing dead leaves and dirt on the tarp, some brush to hide the entrance, and they had a cozy little nest, safe from prying eyes.

Melina must be more exhausted than she was letting on. She made no comment when he led her to the shelter. She just crawled inside, stretched out on the down sleeping bag he'd spread out on a bed of soft boughs, and closed her eyes.

"I'm going to get some sleep, too," he murmured as he crawled in after her. "If, for some reason, something wakes you up that doesn't happen to wake me up, give me a poke, okay?"

One eye opened to stare at him blearily. "In about two minutes, a marching band could go through here and I wouldn't hear it."

He laughed. "Okay, then. We'll rely on my reflexes." Although, as he lay down, doubt in his reflexes flashed through him. He hadn't been out in the field in a very long time, and his system was far from clean from the sedatives and narcotics he'd been doping himself up on for months. Who knew if a threatening noise would wake him from a deep sleep in his current state? He dared not pull a sixty-hour, no-sleep marathon, though. He was alone out here without backup, and there was no telling if the anti-fatigue meds would work properly on him right now—or work at all, for that matter.

Damn, he was a mess. What the hell had he been thinking to let himself get hooked on painkillers and muscle relaxants? Hell, he'd even started taking sleeping pills about a month ago.

He set his wristwatch alarm for four hours and closed his eyes.

He must've slept because he dreamed. Disjointed, bloody nightmares of the Afghan ambush and being chased by the animated, dead bodies of his team. No matter how far or fast he ran, their ghosts were always right there behind him, reaching out to him, trying to speak to him. He didn't want to hear what they had to say!

He awoke, agitated and out of breath, disoriented. Where was he? Green half-light filtered down from a tarp overhead, and the cold and damp of lying on the ground had seeped into his bones. His back, unaccustomed to these conditions, was killing him. He glanced at his watch. The alarm wouldn't go off for another fifteen minutes or so. Perfect.

Taking his backpack with him, he crept outside, being careful not to wake Melina. He rummaged around in a side pocket, experiencing a moment of panic when what he sought wasn't immediately obvious. Urgently, he dug around, and then breathed a huge sigh of relief when he came up with the brown plastic bottle. His hands shaking so badly he almost couldn't tear the lid off, he got the bottle open and poured a half-dozen white pills and four pink pills into his palm. He didn't bother with water. He tossed the lot down dry, and closed his eyes in soul-deep relief. The pain hadn't even abated yet, but just the knowing that it was going to be better soon was enough to send sweet freedom singing through his blood. He already felt halfway human again.

He opened his eyes.

And jolted.

A pale face stared at him from beyond the curtain of brush, still and shocked.

Melina.

Crap. She'd seen it all.

Chapter 9

Stark, cold fear washed over Melina. How bad off was he, this man who was supposed to save her family's lives?

No sense hiding from the truth. He'd already seen her staring out at him. He knew that she knew. She crawled outside on her hands and knees and sat back on her haunches to face him. "Just how badly did you hurt your back eight months ago?" she asked matter-of-factly.

"Are you asking as my client or my doctor?" he retorted sharply.

"Both," she replied evenly.

He shrugged. "Bad enough. It may never be right."

"What exactly did you do to it?"

"You already saw the scar. I was shot. And then I crawled around on it for a couple of days. It got infected, and the surgeons who removed the bullet had to take out a chunk of meat, too."

"How did you get shot?"

His gaze clouded over with painful memories. She'd meant the question in a technical sense…how close was the shooter, what angle had the bullet entered his body…but he seemed to be thinking of more than that. But whatever was on his mind, he didn't answer her.

Okay, then. Not gonna be the world's most cooperative patient.

"I can't help if you won't talk to me."

He snorted with what was supposed to pass as laughter, but came out sounding more like a gasp of pain to her. "I've lost count of the people who've said that exact line to me over the past few months."

"They're right."

He glanced up at her, his gaze piercing her with its power. "I'm aware of that."

This was no simple guy with a painful secret. This was a warrior in his prime. A man of authority and responsibility. Used to being in complete control, of himself and his environment. And clearly, he was not adapting well to not being in control over this.

She replied dryly, "I gather from that look that you've declined to answer any of them?"

His gaze narrowed even further.

"I'll take that as a yes." She pondered him thoughtfully. What could mess up a man like him so badly? It was no great feat of logic to figure out he'd been involved in some sort of law enforcement or military profession until very recently.

She asked neutrally, "Did the bad guy get away when you got shot?"

He jolted. Not the directions his thoughts had been running, clearly. And just as clearly, he didn't like the question. "Thanks, Doc, but I don't need any more people like you poking around inside my head."

She smiled lightly. "So, you've become lovers with all of your doctors? I would have to object to the blurring of the patient-client boundary implied by sleeping with your physicians."

He turned away from her sharply. "Enough already. I didn't sleep with any of them."

"Then please don't lump me with them." When he continued to stare into space in stony silence, she probed again. "Okay, so we're not talking about what happened to the bad guy. What happened to your partner or partners?"

The response was incredible. He didn't move so much as a muscle. And yet, all of a sudden, waves of rage and grief poured off of him so forcefully they all but knocked her over.

And it all clicked in her head. His comments about not deserving to be happy or to live…his deep sense of responsibility…that terrible scar…his utter refusal to talk…

Survivor's guilt.

Somebody he'd worked with, maybe even led, had died. And he, while terribly injured, had lived.

She asked lightly, gently, "So, just out of curiosity, have you ever heard of a thing called survivor's guilt?"

His gaze narrowed. "Free psychoanalysis was not part of this deal. And besides, that's none of your damned business."

Damn. He was not going to cut her any slack, even if they'd made mind-blowing love together and bared their souls to one another. She hated to hurt him, but her gut and her training suggested a little shock therapy might be in order.

Her gaze narrowed back. "My neck's on the line here, sport. And whether you want to admit it or not, you're in trouble. If you want to crawl into a hole and kill yourself after this delivery is done, that's your affair. But right now my life and the lives of my parents and brother are in your hands. The state of your head damned well is my business."

His glare flickered briefly and he had the good grace to look away. Score one for her.

She continued, "You, my friend, present every symptom in the book of survivor's guilt."

He reared back at that. "I am *not* a head case."

"I never said you were. You've suffered terrible wounds, both physical and emotional. You shouldn't underestimate either."

He snorted. "I'm the one popping painkillers and sweating bullets over whether or not I can do this mission."

"Your body is only part of the equation. What about your soul? I've looked into your eyes, John. I've seen your pain. Please don't turn away from me." She would've added that she wanted to help, but it sounded too doctorish in her ears, and he'd clearly had his fill of platitudes from medical professionals. She had to keep this real. It had to stay personal and private between them.

He crossed his arms, his body language screaming defensiveness. "I hate to burst your bubble, Sigmund, but we don't have time for me to go through a couple months of counseling before we continue with this mission."

She shook her head. "This won't be a project for a few months, John. You'll need long-term and qualified counseling to deal with these issues."

He threw up his hands. "Great. Just what I need. Years of shrinks poking around inside my noggin! So much for the rest of my career."

She asked reasonably, "What's more important? Your career or your life?"

He stared at her in angry silence.

Yup. Survivor's guilt all the way. He didn't value his life at more than a plug nickel at the moment. She shrugged. "I'm not trying to tell you what to do. It's your life. Your decision. But I do have a right to ask if you're going to be able to do what needs to be done for me and my family."

He stared at her a long time, the look in his eyes grumpy and bordering on rebellious. She did her best to let all the compassion and calm acceptance she could muster seep into her own steady gaze. She dared not look away from him right now. He'd leap all over any show of weakness from her, and she needed him to face this thing head-on and not turn away from it. She didn't know a blessed thing about sneaky missions and intelligence briefings, or the covert insertion stuff he'd talked to his buddies about earlier, but she did know he wouldn't be good for a damned thing if he didn't at least start to deal with his guilt, and soon.

"We need to get going," he finally said woodenly.

She sighed and nodded. "Okay."

"You rest. I'll pack up and fix us a bite to eat."

She watched in silence as he took down the tarp and packed it away. He sat down on the other end of her log and passed her a steaming pouch of…something.

"Uhh, John, what am I supposed to do with this?"

"Eat it."

She recoiled in horror. A handwarmer, yes, but a meal? No way! She took a cautious sniff. "What is it?"

"Freeze-dried chili mac," he replied cheerily enough to rouse her suspicions. He waved his steaming pouch. "Or you can have my beanie weenies if you like…but they give most people gas like crazy."

She answered dryly, "Thanks, but I think I'll pass on the beans." She poked her plastic spoon at the glop in her bag. Bracing herself, she blew on a bit of it and gingerly put it in her mouth. It wasn't bad in a better-than-nothing way, but gourmet fare it was not. However, she needed the calories if today's hike was going to be anything like last night's marathon from hell. Of course, she didn't have any right to complain if he dragged her up and down the mountainsides; after all, he was doing this at her request to save her family.

She finished choking down the chili mac. By about halfway through the freeze-dried meal, it actually started to taste decent. She cringed to imagine how many taste buds she'd killed to arrive at this state of culinary acceptance.

John efficiently collected their trash and stowed it in his pack. He pointed the way for her to walk up the hill, while he walked backward behind her, fussing periodically. Finally, she stopped and turned around to face him. "What *are* you doing?"

"Erasing our trail."

"You don't plan to make the rest of this trek backward, do you?" she asked in surprise.

He laughed. "No. I'm just making it hard for an amateur to follow us. We don't have time for me to completely counter-track our passage."

"Counter-track?"

He nodded. "That's where I erase our trail so that even a professional tracker can't follow us."

"Why are you messing with our trail at all? Don't the bad guys already know we're coming?"

"Our bad guys aren't necessarily the only fish in the pond out here."

"Oh, good Lord. Are you saying we may have to fight off other bandits before we reach our own personal bandits?"

He grinned widely at that one. "Something like that. I'm hoping that the very act of halfway hiding our trail will deter the casual bandit from fooling with us. There are some truly serious bad guys out here, and I expect the local yokels will want to avoid tangling with the big sharks."

"So you're basically trying to make our trail look like a…a big shark's."

"Exactly." He beamed at her.

"You live in a very strange universe, John Hollister."

His grin widened as he dragged a bundle of twigs across a patch of dirt. "Welcome to my world, darlin'."

Geez. No wonder the guy was a mess. Except he didn't strike her as the type to fall apart. Most of the time he was so strong and centered and mature, like he solidly knew who and what he was and why he existed. But then she'd catch a glimpse of that shadow in his eyes, a vast, empty place of pain and loss. Something really terrible had happened to him. She almost would rather not know what could have rattled a man like him so badly. She was by no means qualified to take on his demons, but unfortunately, she might be all John had. She wouldn't presume to consider herself his soul mate or the love of his life, but she was his lover for now. Hopefully, that would count for something. Like it or not, it was up to her alone to throw the guy a lifeline.

She waited until they'd hiked all day and half the night and had crawled once more into a tiny pup-tent affair that John had rigged up. It was drizzling on and off outside, but he'd managed to find them a dry spot to lie down and had rigged the tarp to keep the rain off them. Clever man. Handy to have around.

To his credit and to her encouragement, he lay down first and then stretched an arm out to her, offering his shoulder for her to sleep on. Given the sharp bite to the air tonight, she was all over cuddling up to his big, warm body.

Once she had her arm and a leg tossed across him, trapping him in place, she launched her first life line at him.

She murmured casually, "How did you get shot, John?"

He turned to stone beneath her. Right there, a full-body transformation to granite. Cold and hard and unyielding. His silence was deafening.

"You need to tell someone. And hey, you've already shared your body and soul with me." She added winningly, "I know about your guilt problem and I haven't run away."

"You can't run away," he bit out.

"Maybe. But I could also have pretended not to notice it, or I could have blown it off as no big deal. But I called it what it is and I still don't hate you."

The tension humming through him was terrible. Yup. She'd

put her finger exactly on the heart of the issue. As she'd suspected. Whatever incident had injured his back was also the source of his emotional wounds. He'd linked the two together. Physical pain and emotional pain all in one big messy jumble in his noggin.

He let out a long, shuddering sigh. It wasn't an answer, but it was a good sign that the granite had thawed to, oh, brick.

"Talk to me, John. Tell me whatever you want to about your back, about how you hurt it, or how it feels now, something. But you've got to start talking. If you bottle this up inside you forever, it'll eat you alive." She propped herself up on his chest and stared down in the darkness at the indistinct shadow that was his face. He was giving nothing away.

She reached up and ran her fingers lightly through his hair, caressing his broad forehead, and murmured, "I care far too much about you to let that happen without putting up a fight." She repeated herself for emphasis. "I'm *going* to fight it, John. You can help me or you can get in my way, but I'm not letting this thing get the best of you without doing my damnedest to stop it."

"The shrinks say it's normal to spend a period of time not wanting to talk about a trauma."

She snorted. "Not when you're destroying yourself over it." She laid her palm against his stubbly cheek and spoke softly. "You've turned whatever happened inward against yourself. It's long past time you talked about it."

Beneath her hand he shook his head.

"Last night you forced me to talk to you, to tell you my deepest, darkest secret. And I have to admit, John, I feel better having it off my chest. I'm not big enough to physically make you talk, and I can't threaten to abandon you out here like you did me. But John, don't you owe me the same honesty you forced out of me?"

* * *

John stared at Melina in thinly disguised panic. The sky was falling, the trees closing in on him. He couldn't do this! Not here. Not now. He couldn't face his demons, not in the middle of an op. Special Forces missions were hard enough without additional dragons to slay. And no doubt about it, this had turned into a full-blown op. Problem was, he was out here solo with a civilian, and what he really needed was a twelve- or sixteen-man team and a whole lot of firepower.

Was she right? Was she all he had? Was he so far down the road to self-destruction that he had to do this now or kill them both? Hell, he didn't know. He didn't know anything anymore. Melina had turned everything he thought he knew about himself and his life on its head.

But to talk about the ambush…to tear back all the careful layers of insulation he'd built over that wound, to relive the agony…terror shuddered through him at the mere thought of it.

"Melina. What you're saying may make sense. But you don't understand what you're asking of me."

She gazed gently at him. "I think maybe I do understand. You're possibly the strongest man I've ever known—and I'm not talking physically. If something happened that even you can't handle, it scares me to death to imagine what that might be. We can't fix whatever happened, and I don't have the training to begin to help you come to terms with it. But I think we have to face it at least a little—enough to make sure you can hold it together well enough to get through whatever lies ahead of us."

He swore under his breath. Like it or not, his gut was telling him the same thing. He pressed the heels of his hands into his eye sockets. It didn't help the sudden and pounding headache he had.

"You don't have to be all macho to show off for me, you know," she murmured. She added coyly, "You already got the girl."

He grinned lopsidedly at her. "I still have a reputation to maintain, you know."

"Okay. Well, you do your muscle flexing and Neanderthal grunting or whatever it is you do, and I'll try to remember to act suitably impressed. But don't suffer needlessly, okay? Your guilt is accomplishing nothing."

A moment of clarity burst behind his eyelids. But he *did* need to suffer. Deserved to suffer. Was that was this was all about? An elaborate form of self-punishment?

He fell asleep without finding any answers. But when he woke up, squinting into the bright morning light, he actually felt a little better. It was probably just a matter of having gotten a few hours of decent shut-eye. He had to give her credit, though. His rest was entirely her doing. He hadn't slept for squat since the ambush…not until Melina had come into his bed and into his arms.

They went through the now familiar routine of eating breakfast and packing up camp in silence. He was eternally grateful that she didn't feel a need to continuously and mercilessly pick at his emotional scabs.

In a contemplative frame of mind, he hefted the big backpack of gear. He waited while she picked up the small, light rucksack he'd prepared for her, and then he turned to face the trail. "Once we top this ridge, we'll descend into a long valley and hike along its length for the rest of today and most of tomorrow."

Melina nodded, a smile of relief on her face.

"Don't look so happy. The forest is thicker down there and it'll be tough going."

Her face fell. "So we either get no oxygen or no trail?"

"That pretty much sums it up. The good news for you is I'll go first and make a trail."

"Three cheers for macho he-men!"

He grinned over his shoulder at her.

In point of fact, the walk down into the valley was pretty easy, and for several hours, they hiked along in companionable silence. He actually enjoyed losing himself in the simple rhythms of movement. The exercise felt good. It had been a long time since he'd done anything like this. Most of his rehab had been done in sterile, impersonal clinics or gyms. But to get outside, smell the green air, feel the wind on his skin…it was a good thing. Yet another simple gift Melina had brought back into his life.

They had about an hour of light left when they hit the tree line and entered the primeval forest of the remote Andes. Its gloom was mysterious and magical, and under other circumstances, he'd have richly enjoyed the opportunity to pass within its hallowed depths. But as it was, Melina was breathing heavily behind him and they were getting low on water. Should he press on and put a little more distance behind them, or should he go ahead and start looking for a campsite and a stream?

A small sound caught his attention. A twig snapping. Not an odd sound in the woods, but for some reason, it stood the hackles on the back of his neck straight up. He turned sharply to Melina and pressed a cautionary finger against his lips. She froze. He gestured with his hands palm down, pressing down toward the forest floor and then he sank down himself. Thankfully, Mel got the idea and sank down beside him.

She threw him a questioning gaze that needed no hand signals to translate.

He leaned close to her and breathed, "I heard something."

Apparently, she understood that he meant he'd heard something not of these woods, something that didn't belong out there. The two of them listened intently for many long minutes. Nada. No more noises even remotely similar to that snapping twig. And frankly, that worried him more than several more twig cracks would have. If there had been a steady pattern of snaps, he'd know some wild creature was nearby. But no beast of the forest had this much patience.

Something was out there, watching and waiting. Or rather some*one*.

Chapter 10

Melina's gaze darted left and right, frantically seeking their follower. They were so exposed out here! She wanted to crawl over to John and creep inside his shirt, to hide her head until the danger went away and let him take care of everything. Except this whole mess was her problem, not his. He'd already gone above and beyond the call of duty to keep her safe.

After an eternity, John leaned toward her and murmured, "Whoever was out there has gone away or gone to ground."

"Which means what, exactly?"

"We can talk and move again. Whoever's out there isn't going to show himself."

"Now what do we do?"

He shrugged. "Now we press on. We still have to get to the next set of coordinates by tomorrow night."

"Look, John, if this is too much for you, it's okay if you just leave me a map and get out of here."

He snorted heartily. Whether that was indignation or

amusement, she couldn't tell. But it was a definite sound of dismissal of that idea. Color her relieved, but she had to make the offer. She couldn't, in good conscience, guilt him into staying out here with her. He was already laboring under guilt aplenty. Speaking of maps, he pulled out one of his and spread it on the ground between them.

"For the record, we're right here." He pointed out a spot on the map with a felt-tipped pen and made a little black dot on its laminated surface. "This is where we're headed." He stabbed at a red dot already marked on the map. "If something happens to me, take this map and walk out of here. Do *not* proceed to the rendezvous alone. Go back to Pirate Pete's and get more help."

She shrugged noncommittally.

He made a sound of exasperation. "If I'm out of the picture, you're planning to continue without me, aren't you? I'm tellin' you, Mel, if you walk into that camp by yourself, I guarantee you and your family are all dead."

"And I'm telling you, John, they won't kill me right away. They want that drug formula from me. And I'll refuse to give it to them unless they set my family free."

"What if they start torturing your folks in front of you? Can you stand the sound of your parents' screams for hours or days on end? How long are you gonna hold out on them when they start cutting your brother's fingers off?"

She grimaced at the grisly images his words evoked.

"How about when they start cutting *your* fingers off?"

"Enough! I get your point!" she exclaimed, horrified.

"Promise me, Melina. If something happens to me, you'll go get help and not try to finish this thing alone."

Her lips pressed tightly together.

He grabbed her by both shoulders. "Look. I can barely hold it together as it is. On top of everything else, don't add the worry that you'll kill yourself if anything happens to me. I can't handle the idea. I care too much about you, dammit."

Her eyes widened in surprise. For that matter, his did too.

"I came out here knowing full well I was on my way to die. Why can't you wrap your brain around that?" she asked in frustration.

He retorted, "Because I came out here knowing full well that I was going to see you through this thing safe and in one piece. Why can't you wrap your brain around that?"

"It's my choice to make and not yours. My life. My family. My choice."

He stared at her in open exasperation.

"With all due respect," she said gently, "you're not exactly the person to criticize me about self-destructive behavior."

The life, the very color, drained out of his eyes until they were black and bleak. Okay, that had been a low blow to hit him with. But darn it, he had to understand how committed she was to going through with this.

His gaze fell away from hers. He spoke quietly. "I suppose I deserved that." A pause. "We make a hell of a pair, don't we? I'm out here wishing to die and vowing to stay alive long enough to see you through this, and you're out here desperate to stay alive, but determined to throw yourself upon your sword anyway."

She gazed into the mirror of his hopeless gaze and flinched at what she saw of herself reflected back at her. Is that what he saw when he looked into her eyes? It wasn't a pretty sight.

She said quietly. "If it's that important to you, I promise I won't try to finish this thing alone. But John, don't let anything happen to you. I care too much about you, too."

He shrugged and started to turn away, but she grabbed his arm and forced him to look at her. "Why do you want to die? Nothing is worth throwing your life away for except maybe saving someone else's life."

His voice was low, charged. "And when you fail to save someone else's life? Then what?"

She stared at him a long time. So that *was* it. Someone he'd been responsible for had died on his watch, and he was consumed by guilt. That certainly explained a lot.

She chose her words carefully. "You grieve their loss. You acknowledge that we all have a time to live and a time to die. And then you go on with your own life. It's the least you owe the person who died. Nobody wants anyone else to stop living on their account."

"Persons who died. Plural," he bit out.

She didn't want to know the answer, but she had to ask anyway. "How many?"

"Eight. My men. Three of them had wives and kids, for God's sake."

Oh, God. Pain for him was a fist in her stomach that she could barely breathe around. And he'd been carrying that around inside him all this time? Reaching deep for strength for his sake, she asked gently, "Did you force them to do their jobs?"

His hand slashed through the air, cutting her off. "I've been through all that logic crap with the shrinks. The fact remains that they're dead and I'm not. And I'm the one who should be dead, not them."

The agony in his voice was almost more than she could bear. "Promise me something, John."

He glanced up at her, surprised.

"When you get home from this expedition, promise me you'll talk to a counselor. A good one. That you'll stick with it until you work this thing out."

His entire being went still. He was looking at her, but she got the sense he was looking through her, not really seeing her. "The only thing I can promise you is that when I get back home, I'm going to finish what you interrupted the day you walked into the store."

"And what was that?"

"I was in the middle of hanging myself."

She reeled back, stunned. Her arms ached to wrap around him, to pull him close and comfort him like a child. But she sensed that he'd implode if she so much as laid a finger on him right now.

She finally whispered, "Oh, John. I'm so sorry."

"You're sorry? What the hell for?"

"I'm sorry you're in so much pain." And she wasn't talking about his back. She was talking about his heart. But then, she expected he knew that. He stared off into space for a long time, lost in his own private hell. And she sat beside him and ached for him with all her heart.

Eventually, he shook himself and took a deep breath. "This has turned into the damnedest op." After a moment he added resolutely, "C'mon. Let's go."

His strength of will was staggering. How he bore this burden and still managed to put one foot in front of the next, she had no idea. They walked for what felt like forever, until the air was cold enough for her to see her breath in the gathering dusk. It was about the only thing she could see. How John was picking his way through the dense forest undergrowth in this gloom, she hadn't the faintest idea. But his broad back moved steadily in front of her, clearing a way past all obstacles and opening a path of sorts for her.

Twice she thought she felt a faint presence behind her. Both times she considered telling John about it but then decided it was just paranoia kicking in. Both times the sensation went away after a few minutes.

Given the cacophony of unidentified night noises out here, they were far from alone in these mountainous climes. Animals and insects kept up a steady chorus of chirps and squawks and buzzes around them as they marched on through the night. That was undoubtedly what she was hearing. After all, who could possibly manage to follow them through these impossible conditions?

Her watch said it was after 4:00 a.m. when they finally stopped to make camp. While John pitched the tarp, she dug out freeze-dried meals and added salt water to activate a self-heating reaction in the pouches. The combination of calories and something hot in her belly refreshed her, and when they stretched out in their usual position pressed together with her head on his shoulder, sleep eluded her.

After a few minutes, John spoke out of the darkness. "What's on your mind that's keeping you awake?"

"You."

He sighed. "Do we have to get into that again?"

"No. I was just answering your question."

Silence fell between them.

She was surprised when he actually broke the lull. "So what were you thinking about me?"

She allowed her palm to slide across his T-shirt and savored the powerful bulge of muscles beneath the soft cotton. "I was thinking about what a remarkable man you are, and how little I know about you."

He replied dryly, "That must be why you still think I'm remarkable."

She smiled against his neck. "You're too modest. If you don't mind my asking, is there anyone waiting for you back on Timbalo Island?"

He started beneath her. "Hell no! I wouldn't fool around with you if there were anyone else!"

"I'm the one who came on to you. I wouldn't blame you if you had a wife or a girlfriend back home. After all, I plied you with liquor and then stripped down to my thong in front of you."

He lurched beneath her, dumping her on her back and looming over her, propped up on his elbow to stare down at her in the dark. "I realize I've given you very little reason to have a decent opinion of me, but I have my standards. I don't cheat on women—ever. If I'm in a relationship, then I'm loyal to it. End of discussion."

She reached up to stroke his stubble-roughened cheek. "You're a good man, John Hollister."

He closed his eyes and she thought he leaned into her touch for a moment.

She continued, "Why aren't you married, or at least involved with someone? You must have women chasing you all over the place."

He chuckled quietly. "Funny, but I've thought the same thing about you. Why hasn't some guy snapped you up long before now?"

She shrugged. "They see a hot chick that'll look good on their arm and hopefully be wild in the sack. They don't ever see *me*. What's your excuse?"

He nodded sympathetically and replied deadpan, "I know exactly what you mean. Guys pick me up left and right and try to treat me like a trophy girlfriend. I get sick of men just wanting me for my looks."

She burst out laughing and swatted his arm. He continued more soberly, "Seriously, my job forces me to travel so much that I can't see asking any woman to wait for me through it all."

"Do you plan to do this courier work forever?" she asked.

"Nah. I'm getting too old for the wear and tear of it all."

"Do you hope to settle down and have a family when you retire?" She asked the question lightly, smoothly, hoping to slip it past him, disguised in the flow of their banter. But, of course, he was far too smart for that.

"You misunderstand me, Melina. I have no plans for a future past the next few days. Once we've got this mess with your family sorted out, I'm hanging it up for good."

She flinched. Apparently, he meant that literally. The idea of him hanging himself caused her tangible pain. Desperation coursed through her. It wasn't like she could take him by the shoulders and shake some sense into him—he was twice as big and ten times as strong as she was. But there was something she could do to figuratively smack him upside the head.

She looped her arms around his neck. "Then why are you wasting all this time talking when you could be making love with me?"

"That, my dear, is a hell of a good question."

Their mouths merged until the kiss stole her breath away. Their shelter was slightly roomier than the back of the Land Rover, and they were able to stretch out at full length, hence, it was a much easier affair to strip each other of their clothes. The air was cold on her skin, a biting chill that made her tingle even before John's mouth and hands closed upon her.

The air smelled wet and organic, mixing with the musk of their bodies. Normally, she'd be appalled at smelling like she'd just come out of the gym, but it seemed appropriate out here. John rolled onto his back and pulled her on top of him, no doubt cushioning her body from the hard, cold ground. She captured his erection between her thighs, rubbing herself up and down the smooth shaft. He reached up, grasping both of her breasts in his big hands, rolling the nipples beneath his thumbs suggestively.

"Harder," she gasped, squeezing his male flesh between the apex of her thighs.

"Ahh. The lady wants it wild tonight, does she?"

She lifted herself up, poising the tip of him at her feminine opening. "Any complaints?"

His hands skimmed down her belly to grasp her hips firmly. He jerked down, hard, impaling her on him in a single forceful movement. She cried out, just on the verge of pain from the fullness of him deep, deep inside her, pressing tightly against her cervix. He lifted her up and pulled her down again, and she leaned back as much as she could under the low roof, driving herself even further down onto him.

His big hands curled around her buttocks, his fingertips opening the crevice between her cheeks and driving her down and forward onto him. Holding her in place with effortless strength, this time he surged up to meet her. Only by relaxing her internal muscles completely was she able to absorb all of his size without pain. He completely filled her, massive and throbbing deep within her very core.

Thus completely opened to him, he drove up into her relentlessly, pounding into her until she thought he would split her in two. But what a glorious, stretching fullness, on a shaft of velvet-covered steel, burning her up from the inside out. A liquid, languorous shower of pleasure drenched her as her body responded to him. She felt swollen, growing tighter and tighter around him. Or maybe that was her muscles clenching as he steadily drove her out of her mind. A tingling started low, building and building, spreading outward from the point of his penetration. Her breath caught and she gasped for air as the building orgasm climbed her throat, her entire body clenching in anticipation of the moment of release.

And then it broke over her in an electric explosion that zinged all the way to her fingertips and toenails and teeth. She gasped as her entire body spasmed around his, shivering as wave after wave of sensation ripped through her.

He gave her just a moment to catch her breath, and then he was moving again, demanding more from her, sliding already wildly stimulated nerve endings against his slick heat. All of a sudden, another orgasm clawed its way through her, bursting upon her without warning, making her cry aloud with the power of it.

He slapped a hand over her mouth and rolled over abruptly, without breaking his rhythm. Her flesh throbbed around him, milking him of more and yet more pleasure. He matched her rhythm, meeting each of her hip thrusts with one of his own, a collision of desire that rode them both mercilessly.

Gripped by instincts far beyond either of them to fight, let alone control, they mated wildly in the forest with the animals of the night for a serenade, and the earth for a bed, the smell of crushed moss rising around them to mix with the scent of their sex.

Just when she thought she couldn't bear any more, the rhythm of their lovemaking accelerated, and one more orgasm exploded behind her eyes. John's hoarse, muffled shout matched hers and for an instant, she spun out of herself, into the blackness of the night. It wasn't quite a faint, but it was close.

Panting, John collapsed on her, and they struggled together to catch their breath. After a minute, he pressed up onto his elbows with a muttered apology for crushing her. By way of reply, she wrapped a leg around his hips to keep him from going anywhere.

When she could finally speak, she murmured, "There now. Wasn't that a more productive use of your remaining time than talking?"

His forehead dropped to touch hers and he laughed under his breath. "Madam, I concede the point."

Her palms slid across his back, kneading and massaging randomly. He felt utterly relaxed beneath her fingertips, a lion at indolent rest. But then, she was feeling pretty boneless herself at the moment.

He murmured, "Think you can sleep now?"

She smiled up at him. "I could sleep a week with you inside me like this."

He made to draw out of her, but she tightened her leg across his buttocks.

"Honey, if I don't move soon, I'm gonna deprive you of even more sleep tonight."

"And that would be the point, Einstein."

He laughed. "You're going to kill me."

It was as if a bucket of ice water fell over both of them. Finally she replied, “It’s a better way to go then what you have planned for yourself.”

His rueful chuckle curled around her heart, breaking it a little. “It is at that. Making love to the death it is. Last one breathing wins.”

She whispered, “If you play this game right, we both win, John.”

“Ahh, sweet Melina. You’re everything a woman should be. I could love you so easily.”

“Show me how you’d love me.”

And somehow she thought he knew she wasn’t talking about sex.

Chapter 11

When John opened his eyes the next morning, he was immediately aware that something had changed. He took stock quickly. Tarp intact overhead. Trip wires at the entrance to their shelter intact. No sounds out of place in the morning chorus of creatures busily going about their day. Melina peacefully asleep against his shoulder.

Melina.

That woman did things to him that no other woman had ever begun to do to him. And he wasn't talking about the sex. Although she was clearly in a league of her own on that score. He was by no means a Casanova, but he'd bedded his share of women over the years, and not one of them completely blew him away like Mel. She got inside his head. Hell, inside his *heart*. She made him *feel* things when they made love, provoked a host of unfamiliar emotions he had no idea how to begin cataloging.

No doubt about it. She was an extraordinary woman. He'd

ask her to marry him in a minute if he had any intention of staying alive for more than the next few days. But as it was, he didn't harbor any illusions on that score.

A guy named Huayar was the crime boss in this region, and he was infamous for never letting anyone live who'd seen his face. The guy was heavily guarded, smart and vicious. And his men were well equipped, well trained and as casually cruel as their boss. Even if there wasn't already a noose with his name on it, going up against Huayar and his men solo like this—he didn't stand a chance of getting out alive. The trick was going to be to give Melina and her family enough of a head start so the guys from H.O.T. Watch could rescue them before Huayar's men caught them.

Jennifer Blackfoot and company might be very good at what they did, but there was no way she was convincing the Peruvian government to let her insert a full-blown Spec Ops team into the Andes. But, a search-and-rescue team...he could see her pulling off that one. After all, the team would, indeed, have to find and extract the Montez family.

The big problem would be the equipment the H.O.T. Watch team would be allowed to bring with them. In the unlikely event that they were given a green light for a full-scale military operation, they'd roll in with gun ships and choppers, predator drones and missiles, and Huayar and his men would be blasted back to the last ice age. But if the H.O.T. Watch guys had to come in as an S&R team, they'd only be allowed the weapons and ammunition they could carry on their backs. Taking on Huayar and his men in a straight-up fight would be a much dicier proposition.

And by himself, with four civilians dragging him down, the only real weapons he had were his brains...and his life. Huayar wouldn't expect him to be willing to die, and that was his lone ace in the hole. Huayar was no stranger to American soldiers. He would assume that John had a healthy desire to live and would predict John's actions based on that assumption. He'd get one chance to surprise Huayar. He only hoped it would be enough.

Melina shifted against him, murmuring in her sleep. What was she dreaming about? The two of them and the love they'd made last night, maybe? She smiled against his shoulder and then settled back into slumber.

Unfortunately, it was time for them to get going. They still had a long march today to reach the rendezvous point by sunset. Despite his big words about getting there whenever they got there, he wanted to get to Huayar's camp as quickly as possible so he had time to scope out the area, and do a little surveillance before he and Melina made contact with the bandit.

He leaned down to kiss her smooth brow. "Morning, sweetheart."

"Mmm." She protested sleepily and snuggled closer against his shoulder. He knew the feeling. He'd love to lie here with her for a week or so, just resting and absorbing her into him. But the clock was ticking.

Always his enemy, but even more so now, time was slipping away from him. For the past eight months, each moment had been a dragging eternity. But now that the end was approaching, it was flying through his fingers like windblown sand. A moment's regret for what he must do stabbed him. If only things could be different—

He cut off the thought sharply, before it could take root inside his brain. His path was set, dammit. Now his job was simply to walk it. No use questioning it at this late juncture.

Melina sat up beside him, stretching lazily, nude and beautiful. Her skin was a delicious golden-caramel color he couldn't get enough of. She leaned forward, peeking out the end of the tent. "Looks like we're in for a warm day."

"It'll be sticky, too. Dress lightly, but keep out a jacket. It'll cool off once we head back up into the mountains."

She groaned in anticipation of an uphill trek.

He commented, "At least we're burning through our supplies and lightening the load."

Her gaze clouded at the reminder that they were nearing the end of their journey.

"The green dot on the map is where we left the Land Rover. There's enough food in my pack for you and your family to walk out to the car. You'll need to collect water after the first day or so and use the water purification tablets on it. Oh, and remind me to show you how my satellite phone works. If you get in trouble, you can use it to call in help."

She glanced over her shoulder at him, frowning. "Why won't you use it to call in help for us?"

"Odds are good I won't make it out of this, Mel. It'll be up to you and your family to get yourselves out of here."

She burst out, "Don't say that! God, it makes me crazy when you talk like that!"

He pressed his lips together. It was the truth whether she liked it or not.

Wordlessly, he disabled the trip wires. They crawled outside, dressed, and ate in strained silence. He'd like to comfort her, to tell her it would be all right. He appreciated her concern, he really did. But she knew as well as he did that planning for anything other than his death on this op would be a lie.

She picked up her pack and slung it over her shoulders, still giving him the silent treatment. He didn't bug her. After all, he'd earned it. He shouldered his own pack and headed out. The remainder of the morning was an easy walk. But then they turned east and started the long trek up and out of the valley. The going was indeed rough, with both steep slopes and heavy undergrowth to contend with. The altitude was starting to get to him, and it surely had to be getting to Melina. But she never uttered a word of complaint. He had to give her credit. She was one tough lady. Not many civilians, male or female, could endure the hardships of an expedition like this, let alone maintain a decent attitude about it. Of course, in comparison to what awaited her if she handed herself over to Huayar, the discomfort of a hike through the woods was small potatoes. And Melina seemed to know that.

In mid-afternoon, he called a halt for them to eat and rest. Over yet another tasteless mush of reconstituted calories—this time optimistically labeled tuna noodle delight—he broke the long silence between them. "What do you know about Geraldo Huayar?"

Worry clouded her gaze. "It's not possible to be near the drug world and not be aware of him."

"Do you know anything about how he operates?"

She shrugged. "I assume he's about like any other drug lord. He controls a large farming, manufacturing and distribution network and maintains his position at the top of the heap by a combination of violence and coercion."

"That's not a bad start. But there are a few more things you need to know about him. He's obsessed with people not knowing what he looks like. He probably travels in normal society occasionally and wants the anonymity. Some people speculate that he may have a family squirreled away somewhere that he likes to visit now and again."

Melina continued to eat, studying him quietly as he spoke.

"Huayar's also a sadist. He enjoys causing pain. He generally tortures hookers to death in the course of having sex with him, and he often conducts his own beatings and interrogations of people who owe him money or cross him. He's a particular fan of cutting off body parts."

She flinched at that one.

"You don't ever want to cross the guy, but it's also vital not to show fear to him. He reacts to it like a hyena. It drives him into a violent frenzy. Show him fear and he'll eat you alive."

"Why are you telling me all this?" she asked curiously.

He shrugged. "Just in case."

"In case what?"

He looked up at her candidly. "In case things don't go well and you end up spending some time with him before my friends can get there and rescue you."

"Your friends?"

He gestured at the phone lying on the fallen log beside him. "My people know you and your family are out here. Not only are you American citizens, but you're also innocent victims of kidnapping and extortion. They'll come get you."

"Who are your friends, exactly?"

The answer to that was classified. And given that there was a real possibility exactly that information would be tortured out of her before this was all said and done, he dared not give her the real answer.

He'd hesitated too long, though, for she said, "I get the message. The less I know, the better."

"I'm sorry." He threw her a regretful look. "I'd tell you under any other circumstances but these. Just trust me. My buddies know their stuff. They can get you and your family out of here." Uncomfortable with the subject, he asked, "Do you remember the phone number I told you to memorize?"

She recited the phone number to a blind line that would be rerouted through a series of remote, untraceable routers to H.O.T. Watch Ops. Even if Huayar extracted it from her, it wouldn't help him locate the facility. And if the guy or any of his men ever managed to show up at Pirate Pete's, they'd be wiped off the face of the earth without a trace.

"How much longer?" Melina asked.

He didn't need to ask until what. She was talking about when they'd reach Huayar's camp.

"We'll get there right around sunset. But we're not strolling in there tonight. I'm going to do a little recon and get the lay of the land before either of us show ourselves. Tomorrow will be soon enough to do this deal."

She looked him in the eye for the first time all day. "So we've got one more night, then."

The words echoed through him with the finality of a jury verdict. One more night. It was hard to fathom that his pain was almost over. Just a week ago, he'd felt nothing at all when considering his death, now he felt a mixture of relief and loss.

They walked until nearly sunset, topping the last ridge and beginning the long run into Huayar's hidden valley. He slowed their pace considerably, paying more attention to silence and stealth than speedy progress.

Melina obviously sensed that they were nearing their target, for she grew silent too, even placing her feet more quietly behind him. He began to keep an eye out for a likely hiding place. It was nearly full dark when he spotted what he was looking for—a tiny gully running perpendicular to their path of travel, most blocked by brush and heavy undergrowth.

"Try not to rub against the branches in here," he murmured. "We don't want to leave threads or other signs of our passage." It was a tall order to ask of an untrained civilian, but he went slow and helped her by holding up ropes of thorny vines and brambles for her to scramble under.

Before too long, they'd worked their way sufficiently far up the gully for his satisfaction. He stopped, and Melina panted quietly behind him. "Okay?" he breathed.

She nodded, probably too winded to talk. Which was just as well. They were within shouting distance of Huayar's outer defenses if John had guessed correctly as to where the guy had deployed his forces.

Tonight, he built a combat hide—a small hollow dug out of the ground with a camouflaged tarp slung across it at ground level. It was low and damp and uncomfortable, but it was invisible, and that was the whole point.

He passed Melina a full canteen and two power bars packed with protein and nearly two thousand calories apiece. Those should hold her for the next few hours. "I'm going to head out and take a look around. I expect to be out most of the night. You stay here, okay? I swear, I'll come back for you."

Her eyes went bigger and darker than usual. She nodded soberly. "I gather there's no chance of talking you into taking me with you?"

He reached into his pack and pulled out three tubes of grease paint and began methodically covering all his exposed flesh in shades of green and black. He glanced over at her as he tied a ragged bandanna around his head. "I've got to be seriously sneaky tonight, and you have no training in that. Besides, it'll mostly entail lying on the ground staring at a bunch of tents with sleeping people in them. As exciting as reconnaissance and surveillance might sound, the truth is they're crashingly boring most of the time."

She looked crestfallen, but thankfully not rebellious.

"Rest and gather your strength tonight, Mel. Tomorrow we'll get your family back, and then all of you will need to hump out of here as fast as you can."

That put a spark in her otherwise terrified gaze. He turned to leave, but she placed a soft hand upon his arm. He stopped and looked down at her.

"Thank you, John. For everything. For making this trip with me. For taking care of me. For letting me into your heart."

Oh, for crying out loud. That was actually a lump trying to form in the back of his throat! He nodded tersely and looked away from her. He spoke under his breath at a point just beyond her right shoulder. "It might even be daylight before I come back. If I'm not back by sunset tomorrow, wait till full dark and then make your way out of here, back to the Land Rover. I've marked the easiest course for you on this map." He shoved the folded map and a spare compass into her hands.

"Come back to me," she said softly.

He glanced over long enough to make brief eye contact with her. Her gaze was unnaturally bright with tears. As hard as he was trying to keep this all business, he couldn't help reacting to her distress. He murmured gently, "This isn't goodbye forever, sweetheart. I'm just going out to take a peek at the layout of Huayar's camp."

"It'll be goodbye forever soon enough," she sobbed under her breath.

He winced. Damn, he wished she wasn't so good at getting under his skin. Women's tears hadn't bothered him for a very long time. But then, they didn't often cry for him, either. Cursing under his breath, he turned and strode out of their secret camp.

As he'd expected, Huayar's camp was at the far end of the valley, backed up against a monstrous stone cliff that made approach from the north nearly impossible. He dropped to his belly and slithered past the first line of sentries, who were spaced too far apart to be effective—case in point, the ease with which he'd slipped between them.

The second layer of defenders were obviously not rank amateurs being broken in to sitting watch in the woods. These guys were better armed, more alert and much more closely spaced along the camp's security perimeter. John took his time easing down the line of men, counting them and taking note of their armaments and positions.

On his second pass of the line, one of the men had turned away from his post to take a piss against a tree, and John took advantage of the resulting gap to creep past the guy. From here on out, he'd proceed strictly on his belly. Which meant the going would be snail slow.

It was almost an hour later when he slowly pushed aside a large-leafed elephant-ear plant and gazed down at the camp before him. At least two dozen armed men and women lounged about. Relaxed though they might appear, he had no illusions on that score. They could be in full-combat mode in as long as it took to hear a gunshot or a sharply worded command.

The camp was laid out in two roughly concentric circles. The smaller sleeping shacks formed the outer ring, and the larger communal spaces occupied a series of tents and crude buildings in the inner ring. The only exceptions were two slightly more solid buildings standing side by side at the very back of the camp...no doubt the drug lab and Huayar's personal quarters. They would be the two most valuable facilities out here, hence, the most protected.

He studied the traffic flow of bandits for the next hour, trying to figure out where Melina's family was being held. There was no sign of any hostages out here, which meant they were inside one of the structures. He pondered the odds that they were in the drug lab, but ruled it out. Huayar was too cautious to take a chance on the family members seeing his production operation and then possibly escaping and carrying tales to his enemies.

Surely, he wouldn't keep prisoners in his home. Not unless he was already torturing them for his own entertainment. And from his two contacts with Huayar's men so far, John had gotten the distinct impression that the bandit had yet to start cutting on the Montez family. So, they had to be somewhere else. Two other structures were heavily guarded and skirted around by most of the bandits...he'd lay odds one was a stash of weapons and ammunition, and the other probably housed Huayar's prisoners. He needed to get closer to those two buildings and take a closer look. He had a 50/50 shot of picking the one with the Montez family in it. Left or right?

He took off crawling to his right because the ground cover looked heaviest that way. He'd almost reached his goal when a sudden presence behind him made him freeze in his tracks. What the—?

Chapter 12

Melina curled up on her side, failing to get comfortable on the hard ground. She missed John's shoulder. Heck, she missed him. How long she lay there listening to the sounds of the night, she didn't know. But it was a long time. Eventually, fatigue and the altitude caught up with her and her eyes drifted closed.

She dreamed of hangmen's nooses and bleak, gray-blue eyes staring straight through her. She woke up with tears on her cheeks. Damn him! Why wouldn't he reconsider his decision to kill himself? Didn't he care enough about her not to rake her over the emotional coals like this? She raged silently into the night, crying and screaming inside her mind. It accomplished nothing except making her eyes puffy and her heart sore. He was being selfish and immature and whatever the male equivalent of a drama queen was! If he were here right now, she'd smack him around and tell him to quit acting like some damned martyr. Didn't he understand that she needed him?

Eventually, her fury gave way to helplessness. There wasn't a blessed thing she could do to talk him out of his decision to kill himself. It was a stark reminder of the solitary journey life ultimately could be. She had to walk her path and he had to walk his. She had no more control over him at the end of the day than he had over her. But then, she'd hoped what they were building between them wasn't about control. She'd hoped it was about something deeper. Something more enduring. Something like...love.

She snorted into the sweatshirt serving as her pillow at that one. Love. Right. He loved her a hell of a lot if he was still determined to kill himself after all they'd shared with each other. If he was really that blind, maybe she was better off without him anyway.

But it was a bitter pill to swallow.

Who'd have guessed? She hadn't allowed herself to care for someone in years, and when she finally did, she picked a man so absorbed in his own misery he couldn't see past the end of his sorry nose. But then, maybe that was the point. Maybe she'd allowed herself to have feelings for him because there was no chance of him reciprocating her feelings for her. He was utterly safe for her to care about.

Okay, that was messed up. She was messed up.

Not like *that* was any big newsflash. After all, she was out here with the intent to trade her life for those of her parents and brother. At least there was a certain nobility to her sacrifice.

She jolted awake sometime later, chilled to the bone and panicked. Something was pressing over her mouth, cutting off her breathing. She grabbed for the hand, clawing frantically at it.

"Easy, darlin'," John breathed from very nearby.

The cobwebs cleared from her brain, albeit sluggishly. That had been possibly the worst night's sleep—or lack of it—in her entire life. She stared up at him and he cocked a questioning eyebrow at her. She nodded from beneath his hand. Yes, she was all here, now. She wouldn't scream.

He lifted his hand away from her mouth, cautiously.

She mouthed, "Can we talk?"

"We can whisper," he whispered.

"Well? Did you see them? Are they all right? How soon can we go get my family?"

"I saw them briefly. They were asleep under blankets, so I didn't see much about their condition. But they didn't look tortured."

She flinched. How did tortured people look anyway? She supposed they would be bruised and maybe bloody. They must get a really haunted look in their eyes, too. The idea of her parents looking like that nearly made her choke.

"Hey, they're alive," John interrupted as a panic attack threatened to take hold of her. The blunt observation shocked some sense back into her. There was that. They were alive. Something to be thankful for.

"How are we going to get them out?"

He exhaled slowly. "About that…"

Her breath caught at the grim tone in his voice. This wasn't going to be good news.

"It's gonna be tough. Huayar's people are good. Very good. Well armed. Well deployed."

"What's the plan now?" she asked grimly.

"First order of business—lie down and go back to sleep. We're probably gonna have a long night tomorrow."

Go back to sleep! He had to be kidding. But surprisingly enough, when he wedged himself in beside her in the tight space and pulled her into her usual position plastered to his side, she actually did fall back asleep reasonably quickly. She must be more exhausted than she'd realized. But then, emotional roller coasters did that to her. It was part of why she'd steadfastly refused to ride them for all these years. She should've known better. But no. She'd hopped on this runaway thrill ride of her own volition with full knowledge of what a colossal wreck it would turn out to be.

For a final time, Melina woke up, this time of her volition and in her own good time. John lay beside her as usual, his arm holding her close against his side and one of his thighs entangled with hers. It was how they usually slept—like they couldn't get enough of one another.

To wake up beside him like this every morning, for a lifetime of mornings, now that would be heaven…strike that thought. Not happening.

Awareness that this was probably the last time she would ever wake up like this, his heart beating solidly beneath her ear, sent tears scalding down her cheeks. John shifted beneath her and she held back her sobs by force, refusing to give in to the grief. Not yet. There'd be time for that later.

But then his lips moved in her hair, and she was lost. Tears streamed down her face as she rolled over and wrapped her arms around his neck, burying her face in the crook of his shoulder.

"Hey, what's this?" he murmured.

"Don't ask," she mumbled. She didn't need him telling her not to care about him and to get over it. He was killing himself and that was that.

His arms wrapped around her with a depth of tenderness beyond anything she'd ever felt from him before. "Sweetheart. Don't tear yourself up over me. I'm not worth it."

She raised her head, gazing at him blearily. "So help me, John. If you say something like that to me one more time, I'm going to kick your ass."

His eyebrows shot up and a startled chuckle rumbled in his chest beneath her. "Well, okay then."

She glared at him for added emphasis.

He pressed his hand to the back of her head, drawing her down to him for a kiss so sweet it all but melted her innards.

She sipped at him delicately, savoring the faint remnant of toothpaste on his breath. How could a guy who was about to die take time to brush his teeth before bed? The paradoxes of this man drove her crazy!

His palms cupped her cheeks, his fingertips sliding into her hair and drawing her head away from him fractionally. "Thanks," he murmured.

"For what?"

"For caring about me."

"I more than care for—" She broke off. She was *not* going there. She was not making any grand declarations of her feelings to a man who'd throw them away along with his life.

"Aww, baby. I really am a bastard, aren't I?" He drew her close and then gently rolled over, reversing their positions. Slowly, he slid down her body, kissing his way lower, divesting her of her clothes and loving her with hands, and mouth and skin. At one point, he laid his head on her breast, and the two of them just breathed together. Nothing more. Just sharing the most basic act of life, their rib cages rising and falling in perfect synchronicity.

And then his body joined to hers seamlessly, pressing deep within her. Her pulse synched with his, and as he began to move inside her, her hips rose to meet him, finding and matching his rhythm as naturally and perfectly as their breathing.

Their lovemaking was achingly slow, each touch, each look, each caress savored as a precious gift between them. And through it all, she gazed up into his storm-tossed gaze, reading his heart in his eyes all the while. He cared for her, too. Maybe even loved her a little.

The crescendo of their sex built gradually in his eyes, darkening and intensifying until she was looking into the throat of a tornado. His turbulent gaze whirled her up and out of herself, pulling her along with him into a place of air, and light and infinite possibility. A place where they would both live forever and all their cares and woes were lifted away from them, leaving just the two of them, joined as one soul, one heart, one spirit.

A climax of such towering perfection, such unendurable sweetness that it made her weep for joy, broke over them. John's eyes went clear and quiet, as serene now as they had been stormy moments before.

He felt it, too.

For just a moment, an unforgettable instant out of time, the two of them had touched heaven.

Tears rolled silently down her cheeks, unchecked. "Thank you," she whispered.

A faint frown flitted across the stillness of his face and then was gone. "For what? I'm the one who should be thanking you."

"For giving me that gift. I'll never forget it."

He didn't ask what gift she was referring to, and she saw understanding in his eyes. It had been that special a moment for him, too. A perfect moment. Not a bad one to go out on, she supposed.

Too overwhelmed, frankly just too wiped out by it all to summon an ounce of anger, she accepted the inevitable. John was going to do what he was going to do, and it wasn't her fault. She'd given him joy. She'd given him love. She'd given him acceptance. There was nothing more she could offer him. If those weren't enough for him to live for, then he was truly not going to be swayed from his planned path.

And shockingly enough, she could live with that. She didn't like it, but he wasn't going to drag her down with him.

Reality came crashing back in on her with a thunderclap of realization in her head that made her reel. She was planning to do the same thing he was! By a different method, and for vastly different reasons, but she, too, was bent on throwing away her life—which at this late date had turned out to be a pretty wonderful and precious thing indeed, thanks to John.

"I get it now," she breathed.

"Get what?"

"What you've been talking about when you accused me of throwing my life away thoughtlessly. You're right. I didn't realize it until just now. I was so blinded by my need to save my family that I didn't look past Huayar's demand that I sacrifice myself to him."

John stared at her in open shock. "Are you backing out of this crazy scheme, then?" he asked hopefully.

She frowned up at him. "I can't abandon my family. I won't abandon them. But I am willing to listen to other options."

"Finally," he breathed in profound relief. He drew his sleeping bag over them both, and settled back to stare up at the tarp a foot over their heads in the dim, gray light of dawn. "Here are your choices."

She settled against his shoulder, suddenly eager to hear his plan and desperate to find a way to save her family *and* stay alive.

"First, you can make the trade as Huayar has proposed. You walk into his camp, he releases your family, you stay with him and teach him how to make this new drug. Maybe you stick around long enough to help set up and even manage his lab for a while before he kills you. But at the end of the day, he kills you. And then he kills your family. He'll never leave them hanging around in the long term, possibly knowing what he looks like. Bottom line, you'll all die, and Huayar gets his drug formula."

She winced at hearing her original plan and its inevitable conclusion laid out so baldly. She'd never really thought past getting her family released to what would happen next.

"Second choice, you and I mount some sort of covert rescue op to see if we can pull out your family and not hand you over to Huayar at all. I have to be honest with you. The odds of us succeeding are not high. Huayar's men know what they're doing, and their security is tight. Not airtight, mind you, but definitely tight."

She nodded, wincing.

"Behind door number three, we have some sort of hybrid plan between these two."

"Like what?"

He shrugged. "We maybe let you walk into Huayar's camp and use your presence there as a distraction while I go in from the back and try to free your family. Then, once I've got them clear of the camp, I come back for you."

"What are the odds on that scheme?"

He exhaled heavily. "Not that great. If your family gets away but you stay in Huayar's custody, he'll try to cut his losses and force you into giving him the drug formula at a minimum. Then, he's likely to come after your family again and try to recapture them."

She shuddered. "Does there happen to be another choice?"

John was silent for a long time. "Yeah. There's another option."

"Which is?" she demanded impatiently.

"I walk into Huayar's camp and offer myself as a hostage in your family's place. They get released, and he uses me as leverage to keep you in line and get you to cough up the formula."

She frowned. "But isn't the point not to give him the formula?"

He nodded grimly. "You won't hand over the formula. You'll let him do whatever he wants to me, and you won't give him the formula. Huayar doesn't know I'm prepared and, in fact, *planning* to die. He'll assume he can torture and mutilate me, and you'll buckle and give him what he wants."

"But John—" she started to exclaim.

He clapped a hand over her mouth. "Keep your voice down," he snapped.

She nodded her understanding and he pulled his palm away

from her face. "But John!" she exclaimed under her breath. "I can't let you hand yourself over to him like that! He'll do horrible things to you!"

John nodded, his chin lightly rubbing her hair.

"No way," she declared forcefully, if quietly.

"It's the best option. Your family gets away, Huayar doesn't get the formula right away. It'll give my buddies time to get there and rescue you. If you need to, you can buy more time by giving him fake formulas or claiming to need to perfect the formula you've got."

"But I do need to perfect it—"

He cut her off gently. "I can probably hold out for two days. Maybe three. You'll only need to buy a day or two more before my buddies get here in quantity and pull you out. Five days. If you can just stay alive for that long, you should walk out of this thing alive, along with your family. I get my fitting ending, and you all get your lives back."

She didn't stop to think about what she was doing. She balled up her fist and jammed it into his gut as hard as she could. He jerked up off the ground, grunting in surprise and pain.

"What'd you do that for?" he complained.

"I told you to quit making stupid remarks about deserving to die," she groused back.

Unaccountably, he unfolded from around her fist, stretching back out beneath her. His body began to shake suspiciously. She frowned for a moment and then realized he was laughing. Whether it was out of despair or actual humor, she couldn't tell. But either way, it was better than his calm, cool, controlled martyr act.

"I'm telling you, Mel, this is the best option. I'll pop a big bottle of pain pills before I go. Even without the pills, I can take a world of pain. It's part of my Special Forces training. I can buy your family days to get away from here before Huayar realizes he's made a mistake. I'll have the guys from

Pirate Pete's pick your family up. They have connections and can arrange for you and your family to go far, far away and get new identities, new lives."

"You're asking me to hand you over to a madman to let him do his worst to you."

He shrugged. "Death is death. The means isn't all that critical."

She closed her eyes. How could a moment of such perfection degenerate into this so fast? Could she seriously allow John to throw himself upon his sword for her? Could she bear to let him be tortured and mutilated, undoubtedly before her eyes? No matter that he was volunteering for the job, could she let another human being die for her?

Chapter 13

John stared deep into Melina's eyes, a little stunned himself that he was making the offer. A year ago, he'd never have dreamed that he could find himself in this situation. He'd always known on an intellectual level that there were principles and beliefs worth dying for. And he'd discovered in the past eight months that there were certain events, even certain feelings, that made death preferable to going on living.

But he'd never, ever dreamed he'd meet a woman he'd be willing to die for, no questions asked, no hesitation, no doubts in his mind.

Was this love?

The question exploded across his mind, a comet burning bright across the black landscape of his soul. The answer followed immediately, as sure and clear as his willingness to give his life for Melina. How could it be anything else? He loved her. With every fiber of his being. Beyond all reason, without reservations, heart and soul. She knew the worst of him, and had seen his devastating weakness and fatal flaws. She'd gazed into the darkest corners of his soul, and not only had she not flinched, but she'd dared to like him, maybe even to love him a little. The sheer humanity of her acceptance of him as he was took his breath away. She was an extraordinary woman. How could he not love her?

He didn't relish the idea of being tortured to death, and he had faith that Huayar would make him suffer to a degree he couldn't even begin to imagine. After all, the guy was famed as an artiste at inflicting pain. But to submit himself to Huayar for Melina? Shockingly, he embraced the opportunity to show her his love.

She interrupted his train of thought. "John, what are you trying to do by martyring yourself for me? Is this about redemption? About allowing yourself to be punished for living when your men died?"

He frowned up at her. He wished there were more light to see her by. As it was, her face was a collage of shifting gray shadows. Full dawn was still several minutes away. "A few days ago, it would have been about that. But now…"

She propped herself up on his chest and stared down at him intently in the gray half-light. "Now what?"

"Now," he paused, searching for the right words. "Now, it will be a gift. From me to you. You're the most incredible woman I've ever met. You've given me peace, and that's the greatest gift you could possibly have given me. I want to repay you. Give you something back. Something of great worth. If I can give you your family, then my death—as gruesome and painful as it might be—will have been well worth it."

She stared in disbelief. "So you're telling me you want to die to show me how much you care for me?"

"No. I want to give you my life to show you how much I love you."

She lurched and he had to grab onto her and hang on tightly

to keep her from heedlessly leaping to her feet and destroying their shelter.

"John Hollister, that is the dumbest thing I have ever heard another human being say."

Stung, he frowned at her. "I just declared my love for you and you're calling me stupid?"

"Absolutely. If you love me, you big, sweet moron, then you *live* for me. Don't die for me!"

Stunned, he pulled back from her—as much as he could in the tight confines of their shelter—to stare at her. Live for her? A shocking concept. He'd been so focused for so long on finding a way to die, that the idea of finding a way to live felt…strange.

Which was odd, given that the entire creed of the Special Forces was to find a way to do the impossible and survive. He and his men had done their damnedest to stay alive at all times. As the team leader, it had been his job to get the mission done, but even more important in his mind had been his mission to bring his men back alive and kicking every time.

He'd been so wrapped up in his men's deaths for all this time that he'd forgotten why it had been such a trauma to him that they died. *Because to them, living had been the most important thing of all.*

Maybe she was right. Maybe it wasn't a fitting tribute to their memories for him to die, too.

He went still at the thought. Physically still, but also emotionally still. Way down deep inside him. The wild carousel he'd been riding round and round stopped whirling for just a moment of clarity.

That single moment of understanding was enough. The words all the counselors, and psychologists and his colleagues had been throwing at him to no avail finally got through. If he wanted to honor his men, then he'd go on living. He'd find a way past the impossible odds of his guilt and grief, and he'd go on. For them.

The terrible tension in Melina's face drained away. She must have sensed the direction of his thoughts. She relaxed on top of him, still propped on her elbows, gazing down at him. That might even be the beginning of a relieved smile flirting with the corners of her mouth.

He let out a long, slow breath. "I think I get it now."

"Praise the Lord," she replied fervently. "I really wasn't looking forward to trying to whack you upside the head with a heavy object. But I was about to resort to that."

Gratitude flooded him. And something else…was that joy? That she cared enough about him to go to all this trouble? It was a humbling thought. "I don't deserve you," he mumbled.

She laughed under her breath. "I don't know. I think maybe we deserve each other."

"I have a deal to offer you," he said soberly.

She matched his tone when she replied cautiously, "What's that?"

"I'll do my best to walk out of this mess alive if you will."

She stared at him for a long time, doubt swimming in her gaze.

Usually the soul of patience, he couldn't stand the suspense of waiting for her answer. He gave her a nudge to tip the scales his way. "I promise we'll do our damnedest to get your family out of here safe and sound, but let's both try to stay alive in the process."

That did it. She nodded in quick agreement. "I don't know if what you're offering is possible, but I'm willing to try."

They gazed candidly into each other's eyes for what seemed like forever. The promise of a lifetime leaped between them, of a million tiny stitches weaving together into a single quilt that would warm them in its love until time ended. They had no need for words. There was nothing left to say. They loved one another, and they would live for each other.

Finally, reluctantly, John broke the silence. "We have a small problem."

"What's that?" she murmured.

"Everything I've done so far on this mission has been on the assumption that we were both coming up here to die."

"And?"

"If the object is now, as you succinctly put it, for us morons to live, then we're not exactly ideally situated to make that happen."

She grinned down at him. "Who are you calling a moron, buddy?"

He grinned back. "Any woman who would love a wreck like me might just qualify for the title."

She reached up to run her fingers through his thick hair. "I'm just the only one to come along who was smart enough to see the potential in you."

"Thank God for that." He paused, then added, "Thank God for you."

She smiled serenely at him. "I have complete faith in you, John. You'll figure out a way for us to rescue my family and get us out of this alive—all of us."

He frowned. It was a tall order. After all, he'd led them right into the lion's den. Heck, the lion's jaws. They were under-equipped and under-manned…by a lot…for what she was asking of him. Not to mention time was short. Huayar wouldn't wait more than a another day or so before he decided that Melina had welshed on her end of the deal. No telling what Huayar would do to her family in that event. He, for one, didn't want to find out what the guy would do.

John gently put Melina aside and sat up. He had to think up a plan, and fast. Brute force was the last resort of the Special Forces. They'd much rather move into a scenario in complete stealth, do their job with the least possible fuss, and exit as quietly as they came, invisible and undetected. In this case, he and Melina—even assuming she knew how to handle a gun, which he highly doubted—didn't have enough firepower between the two of them to even begin to consider any kind of frontal attack on Huayar and his men. They would have to rescue her family by pure stealth.

At the end of the day, there wasn't much to plan. He'd park Melina somewhere nearby, safe from discovery but close enough to meet up with him and her family when they egressed the area. He'd go in alone. Since he was without any intelligence on the camp beyond what he'd seen earlier, he'd have to improvise as he went. On the plus side, he had a career's worth of experience to draw on. On the minus side, he hadn't been out in the field since the ambush. He was bound to be rusty.

His boss, General Wittenauer, was prone to say he'd rather work with an American Special Forces team on a bad day than any other soldier in the world on a good day. Apparently, that theory got to be put to the test, and he was the guinea pig.

He glanced at his watch—7:00 a.m. He could probably catch a few hours' sleep, but then he'd have to get moving and start his approach to the camp. He'd need to be in place close to the compound before nightfall. He'd need all of the coming night's hours of darkness to rescue Mel's family.

He set his wristwatch alarm to vibrate him awake at noon. He was cutting it close, but he was in lousy physical shape after the past few days' hiking and emotional upheaval, and he needed to be at the top of his game for what he had planned. Melina seemed content to doze beside him as the day heated up and their tiny shelter grew sultry with humidity and body heat. He mumbled instructions to her to wake him if she heard or saw anything at all out of the ordinary, and then he crashed.

When his watch jangled against his wrist, he jolted awake from a surprisingly deep and restful sleep.

"Hey, handsome," she murmured against his neck.

"Hey back atchya, beautiful."

She stretched with feline abandon against his side. "I needed that."

He laughed under his breath. "So did I."

Her hand meandered across his chest, idly at first, then dipping suspiciously lower. He captured her fingertips and carried them to his lips. "It's time to get going, sweetheart."

"No good-luck farewells or lingering kisses?" she murmured in disappointment.

"I wish. But I've got a lot to do before sunset."

"What about me? What do I have to do?"

"We have to find you a hiding spot, and get you tucked out of sight."

"I have to *hide*?" she exclaimed under her breath in disappointment.

"Sorry. But I've got to do this alone." He explained regretfully, "I'm going to draw upon all kinds of tricky Special Forces skills, and an amateur would only get in my way."

She nodded her understanding, and thankfully, didn't protest.

"You will need to be ready to boogie the second I hand your family over to you. I'm going to give you some maps to study with several alternate routes drawn on them. I need you to study those maps like crazy and memorize every nuance of them, every topographic line, every hill and valley, every ridgeline. Your life and your family's lives may depend on you knowing those maps like the back of your hand."

She nodded seriously.

Of course, if all went well, he'd be there to lead them all out, and the exercise in map memorization would be fruitless. But it would keep her busy for a good long time and make her feel useful. And keeping her happily occupied was vital. Civilians with too much time on their hands to think had a tendency to talk themselves into all sorts of trouble, and he really needed her to just sit tight and be patient.

They grabbed a quick bite to eat, refilled their canteens, and packed up their makeshift camp. He carefully erased the signs of their presence, laying down and tamping into place the rolled sod of moss he'd removed before he'd pitched their shelter.

They moved carefully, easing around the south side of the camp to its western margin. The compound's north end butted up against the cliff, and the east side was bounded by a small, but fast-flowing stream. He planned to use the noise of that flowing water to mask his approach to the camp, in fact.

He found a thicket a little way up a steep western slope, and settled her deep in the middle of the jumbled vines and brambles. She was well clear of the camp, out of sight and mostly out of earshot. Her position was readily accessible from the hillside above, too, which was likely to be the direction from which he and her family approached her.

He'd give anything to have radios for the two of them to stay in touch, but he hadn't come out here expecting to run a rescue mission. As it was, maybe it was a good thing she couldn't call him at an awkward moment and blow his cover as he approached Huayar's hideout. Another thing he'd learned about civilians over the years: they tended to babble when they got nervous, and they sucked at radio discipline. The combination had potential to be deadly if they wouldn't shut up and stay off the airwaves at critical moments.

He stepped back to survey Melina in her makeshift hide. He adjusted a few branches, and then nodded his satisfaction. "You're all set, sweetie. Give me until sunrise tomorrow. If I or your family don't meet you here by then, go west as fast as you can until you know you're alone. Call that number I had you memorize and tell the guys what's gone down. They'll come get you."

"But what if—"

"If we don't walk out by tomorrow morning, we're all

dead or about to be dead. Nothing you can do will save us at that point."

Her eyes went big and dark with apprehension. "You have to make this work, John. For us."

For them. The words were like Cupid's arrow straight through his heart, sharp with pain and soothing with balm at the same time. "Honey, I'm gonna do my level best."

She smiled up at him, and he leaned down to kiss her. He paused, inches from her mouth. "Has anyone ever told you how beautiful you are?"

She laughed up at him and reached up behind his neck to drag him down for a kiss. "I love you, John Hollister."

He lifted away from her far enough to gaze down into her warm…loving…eyes. "I love you, too."

Still fresh on their lips, the words flavored their kiss of farewell with unbearable sweetness. They broke the contact with the greatest of reluctance, and it took all the strength of will he had to straighten up and take a step back from her.

"Go get 'em, tiger," she murmured.

He grinned jauntily. "A walk in the park, darlin'."

But when he turned to walk away, a suspicious wetness on his cheeks threatened to smear his greasepaint.

Chapter 14

Melina stared at the maps John had left with her until she could see every last detail of them perfectly in her mind's eye. Much of the terrain she recognized from their trek into this valley, and it helped her to visualize what the various routes John had marked on the map would look like on the way out. She snacked on one of the power bars he'd left her and sipped at one of the bottles of water in her pack.

And she waited.

It was nerve-racking in the extreme to just sit here like this, with no idea what John was doing at this exact moment, not knowing whether her family was all right, or whether Huayar had lost patience with her and decided to kill them all. She told herself a hundred times that Huayar wanted the drug formula bad enough to wait for her to show up, especially since John had made a big deal of the fact that they were going to take their sweet time getting here. It would be all right. It would be all right. It would be…

Although she didn't think it would ever get there, the sun finally began to dip into the west, sliding down toward the line of mountains behind her. She couldn't see the mountains because of the thick canopy of forest overhead, but she felt their massive presence looming, solid and immovable, measuring time in eons her puny human mind couldn't begin to comprehend.

John should be in position near the camp by now. He'd told her his goal was to get close to the camp today, so that as soon as it got dark he could start his move into the compound. She couldn't imagine how he planned to work his way right into the middle of a heavily populated place like that, but he seemed confident he could pull it off. And since their future rested on it, she had faith he was plenty motivated to succeed.

She was so proud of his progress. He really seemed to have turned the corner last night when he finally gave himself permission to consider staying alive. Once he'd made that leap, the rest of it had been easy. He'd figured out immediately that the best way to honor the memories of his fallen comrades was to stay alive and keep their memories alive in his heart. She'd seen the whole argument play out in his wonderfully expressive eyes. She hadn't done half-bad for only having one rotation in medical school in psychiatric counseling. But she still wanted him to talk to a pro when they got home.

She occupied herself for a while imagining moving to Timbalo, the island where Pirate Pete's delivery service was based. It was a sleepy little place, sunny and golden and sexy…with John around, she could definitely see herself living there.

That was, assuming Huayar and company could be persuaded to leave her the heck alone, and she didn't have to go into hiding or take even more drastic measures. She'd hate to undergo plastic surgery or give up all contact with her family after fighting so hard to get them back. But if she'd learned nothing else from John, it was that sometimes extreme measures were necessary to stay alive. After finding him, she'd do whatever it would take to have a future with him.

The sun slid below the mountains, unseen, and the light began to fade around her. The vivid greenery faded to olive, and then to gray. Night creatures began their chorus, and she shrugged into the sweatshirt John had thoughtfully left for her. A macaw screeched nearby and she about had heart failure before she recognized the distinctive caw. But then she settled down once more and began to wait in earnest. John was actually moving into the camp now.

And then she began to worry.

How long she sat there, feeling useless and exposed by turns, she didn't know. Impatience built in her, a restless need to move. To know what was going on. But John had been adamant. She was supposed to stay right here. At all costs. An hour passed. Two. And the tension of waiting became nearly unbearable.

Then the screams began.

They started as a series of indistinct sounds coming from the direction of Huayar's camp, and grew into a horrible sound of fear and pain. Oh, God. Had they discovered John? Her palms broke out in a cold sweat. She prayed fervently that he was safe and still hidden.

But then the screams morphed into something sharper. More urgent. It was definitely the sound of someone in terrible trouble. Her entire body broke out in a cold sweat. Panic made her shaky, and a need to *do something* dug into her until she thought she'd tear her hair out.

The thick vegetation distorted the noise, making it bounce crazily around her until she could hardly tell where it came from. But it was definitely the sound of torture. Was that John? Should she do something? He'd said to stay here. But, if he was in trouble, she couldn't do *nothing*.

He would tell her there wasn't anything she could do. He'd tell her to leave. To save herself. Except everyone she loved was down there in that camp. What did saving herself matter if her parents and her brother and her lover all died?

Another scream split the night. She about leaped out of her skin at the piercing sound of human agony. Ohgodohgodoh-god…

Was that her mother or father? Mike? Now what was she supposed to do? She had to take action. It would kill her not to.

A new scream erupted, louder and even more agonized than the last one. She stood up. Took a step forward, then crouched back into place. Should she…John had said to stay…but someone was in trouble…what could she do…she wouldn't know if she could help until she saw what was going on….

She inched forward, relieved beyond all reason to be moving, to be acting upon the adrenaline pounding frantically through her. She'd just creep a little closer. She'd go slow like John talked about. She'd stick to the shadows, and only go close enough to catch a glimpse of what was going on. She'd be careful.

Thankfully, because of the maps he'd made her study all afternoon, she had little trouble staying oriented as she moved toward Huayar's camp. If she slid to the left a bit, the map showed a high outcropping that overlooked the camp nicely. She should be able to crawl out on it and get a decent view of what was happening below without ever coming much closer to the camp than she was now.

In theory it was an easy task. Except she failed to take into account the paralyzingly thick vegetation, the even more paralyzing open patches of ground, and the sick nausea of fear rumbling in her gut. Every time another scream pierced the night, she lurched, pushing herself to keep moving forward, to set aside her own safety and keep pressing closer to the danger.

How on God's green earth did John do this so casually? It

was a no-brainer to guess that he'd been a soldier of some kind before he got shot. He'd referred to his Special Forces skills just before he left, in fact. Her heart was about to pound right out of her chest, and she was alone and safe in the shadows. What must he be experiencing, down among Huayar's men in the open, without cover to speak of? Please, God, let that not be John down there, his voice growing hoarse from his screams....

Finally, she crouched behind the drooping branches of a tree fern and peered out at the rocky outcropping she'd sought. Yikes. It was really open out there. Only rocks and moss for cover. She shed her backpack and lay down on her belly. She commenced edging forward, and rapidly gained new respect for snails. The further out the ledge she went, the dumber an idea it seemed. She was way exposed out here. But John would've taken a risk like this for her—heck, was taking a greater risk for her at this very minute.

Just a little bit further, and then she'd be able to see down into Huayar's camp. She dragged herself forward a few more inches on her elbows, and then froze, staring down in horror.

A tiny red dot illuminated the top of her right hand. It slid up her arm, across her shirt pocket and disappeared, presumably centering itself somewhere in the middle of her forehead. She dropped flat, breathing hard. Crap. She'd watched enough television shows to know that was a laser sight from a rifle. She waited for the bullet to slam into her entirely vulnerable flesh. But nothing happened.

Her body went hot, then cold. And belatedly, her brain kicked back into gear. That had to be one of Huayar's men. Of course they wouldn't shoot her—Huayar wanted to take her alive! The sniper had probably radioed down to the camp that he'd spotted her. Heck, there was probably a welcoming party of armed men heading for her position right now.

She jumped up and took off running, heedless of the sniper tracking her movements. She had to get back into the trees.

Out of sight. She crashed past the tree fern, not bothering to scoop up her backpack. Bug spray and spare bottles of water were meaningless to her if Huayar's men caught her.

Faint crashing sounds came from behind her.

She put on a new burst of speed. She tried to traverse the steep mountainside on the assumption that Huayar's men would expect her to run downhill. Oh, how tempted she was to barrel down the slope. But she was pretty sure that path spelled disaster.

She slowed down, both from complete lack of oxygen, and because her gut told her silence was more important than speed, now. Her pursuers knew she was out here. They'd comb these woods all night if they had to. This was no longer a chase. It was now a life-or-death game of hide-and-seek.

John crouched in the shadows of one of the sleeping huts, a ramshackle affair of corrugated tin and scrap wood. It would keep rain off the hammocks within, but that was about all that could be said for it.

He clenched his jaw as Huayar continued wielding his knife. The prisoner screamed again, pleading for mercy, and swearing upon a variety of saints that he had not stolen drugs from the latest shipment he'd delivered.

John subsided in the shadows, thinking hard. The drug lord's ploy was transparent. Huayar figured Melina was nearby, hesitating to walk into the camp, and the bastard was giving her something to think about.

John hoped fiercely that Melina was heeding his instructions to sit tight and do nothing. But he had a sinking feeling in his gut that she wasn't. The tortured man's screams were wrenching, and she had to be completely flipped out. She had no way of knowing whether or not that was him or one of her loved ones screaming their head off. He had to get her family out of here, and fast, before she went and did something stupid.

He looked all around. The good news was that the sentries were looking avidly over their shoulders at Huayar's bloody spectacle. John eased forward, gliding silently across an open area and sinking slowly into the shadows of another sleeping hut. The building beyond this one was where Melina's family was being held. He rolled slowly under the nearest hammock and inched his way along the interior wall toward his goal.

Hang on, sweetheart. Don't let the screams get to you. Trust me. Do what I told you to....

Melina crouched, panting, beneath the limbs of a clusia tree. Its round, leathery leaves blocked out the sound of her pursuers, but she had no doubt they were still out there. She could *feel* them closing in on her.

Maybe she should just stop this foolishness and give up. She could raise her hands over her head and walk out of the bush, and tell Huayar's men she'd gotten lost trying to find his camp. She'd followed the screams to the area, but then had gotten scared when someone tried to chase her. If she acted lost and stupid enough, maybe she could sell the explanation to Huayar and his men.

She wanted to shout for John, to beg him to come make it all better like he had so many times already. But she was on her own out here. He'd told her stay put and she hadn't. Except, even knowing she'd be chased like a fugitive, she would still have tried to help him. If nothing else, maybe she'd drawn some men and some attention away from the camp and made his job easier. She had to believe he was still okay, that he was still working on freeing her parents. Any other sequence of events had no meaning for her, because she'd rather die herself than lose her family.

Die herself...

Comprehension flashed across her mind. This was how John felt! This was why he'd been so hell-bent on joining his comrades in death. They'd been family to him, perhaps the only people he really cared about. And he'd lost them. Her own heart bled for his anguish.

Crackling noises in the brush nearby made her freeze, holding her breath. She listened for a long time, determination and doom warring within her. But then her resolve stiffened. If John had promised to fight through the loss of his military family and keep on going for her, surely she owed him no less.

She eyed a sweet gum tree off to her right. If she could get behind that, there was a heavy stand of underbrush she could worm her way into. She eyed the menacing gloom of the forest around her. Nothing moved. A twig snapped, farther away than a few minutes ago. She eased out of her hiding spot. It was now or never.

John eyed the building across the last open space before him. This structure was solidly built with tin siding and small windows perched up high. He'd peered into one of those windows last night and spotted Melina's parents and brother asleep inside. Surely, they were wide-awake now, what with all the screaming and commotion in camp.

He would've preferred to come upon them while they were sleeping—they'd be less likely to give away his presence by some expression of surprise or joy at seeing a rescuer. But, he had to move now. No way would Melina sit out there for long doing nothing, listening to that poor sod scream. She was far too compassionate and empathetic a soul for that.

He waited until Huayar did something that made his prisoner howl like a banshee. Every guard's head turned toward the central clearing, and John used the moment of distraction to glide across the path and into the shadow of the structure. He slid around back to the same window he'd peeked into the night before. Grabbing its sill with his fingertips, he did a slow chin-up to peer inside.

He stared in dismay. Gone! The room was empty. No people. No blankets on the bed. Nothing. He let himself down silently and crouched below the window, thinking.

Huayar had moved his prisoners. This was not good. Not good at all. Huayar had anticipated that someone might try to come in here and rescue Melina's family. Word had obviously gotten back to the bandit that Melina Montez had brought help with her. A potentially competent operator. Damn, damn, damn.

If Huayar was operating on the assumption that his enemy was highly skilled, then the bandit would've taken other security precautions, too…John swore under his breath…like the poor schmuck screaming behind him. All of a sudden, Huayar's choice of torturing some guy tonight took on a whole new significance.

Was this entire scenario an elaborate trap?

Crap. How could it not be? The screaming was meant to lure Melina into the open. Maybe even to give John a plausible cover under which to sneak into the camp and attempt a rescue. And the prisoners had been moved. He'd bet a bundle that if he tried to get into the now-empty room at his back it would be chock-full of booby traps.

He had to get out of here now!

As another scream erupted behind him, John took a quick look around and made a dash for the trees. The vegetation was thin here at the foot of the massive cliff behind the camp, but it was enough. He melted into the shadows, abandoning hours' worth of patient penetration of the encampment. Frustration ground his molars together. He needed more resources, dammit!

Alternate plans flashed through his head almost too fast to process, but one necessity overrode all others. He had to get back to Melina. To let her know that wasn't her brother or her father being tortured. To get her to sit tight and let him come up with another plan.

He moved off to the west, easing around the perimeter of the camp and its inner ring of guards. Now that he took a head count, he noticed that there were more than double the number of guards posted tonight compared to last night. Oh, yeah. The bastard had laid an elaborate trap for them. He had to get to Melina, and fast. She'd fall into Huayar's snare as innocently as a rabbit sticking its head in a hunter's clever lure.

Sit still, Mel. Sit still.

Chapter 15

Melina ran for all she was worth, away from the distant sounds of movement in the jungle. If only John were here, he'd know what to do. Panic was getting the better of her, and despite knowing that this was a bad thing, she couldn't help its creeping advance.

Yet again, breath deserted her, and she stopped in the lee of a large-leafed bush of some kind. The forest felt alive, dozens of eyes peering out of every shadow. At the very edge of her vision, she imagined she saw a vaguely human form materialize out from behind a tree, a shadow within the shadows, and beckon to her.

Just then, crashing sounds erupted behind her and she looked over her shoulder, frantically. She turned back around to that ghostly form, and it was gone. Great. Now she was hallucinating. Must be the lack of oxygen.

Air or no air, she had to get moving. Still gasping from her last sprint, she dashed off again, this time in the general direction of that desperate vision.

John froze in the woods only a few dozen yards beyond the last line of guards. Sweet mother of God, the entire forest was crawling with Huayar's men. They were crashing around like a herd of angry elephants. He dived for cover and quickly pulled handfuls of dead leaves and dirt up over himself as a pair of bandits rushed past.

Definitely looking for something. Or someone.

His stomach dropped like a block of lead. *She'd moved.* She'd approached the camp to try to save him or her father or brother or whoever she thought was doing all that screaming. Huayar's ploy had worked like a charm to draw her out. They must not have found her yet, though, or they wouldn't be bombing around out here trying to flush her out.

Frantically, he tried to send her a telepathic message. *Go to ground, Mel. Find a hiding spot and hunker down. Just. Don't. Run.*

Melina ran until the stitch in her side was so severe she could hardly see, let alone breathe. Not that it mattered. Someone behind her had spotted her and sent up a great shout. It sounded like twenty men were chasing her now. It was only a matter of time until they closed in on her. The sounds of branches breaking and men swearing were within maybe fifty feet of her now.

The jig was up. They were going to catch her.

In the few remaining seconds she had left, she had to think fast. John had said not to show Huayar fear. Ever. Surely, running around like a fox pursued by Huayar's hounds was a colossal statement of terror. She had to take control of this situation, and now.

Quickly, she brushed as much of the dirt and leaves off

herself as she could. She waited until she spotted the first of her pursuers, and then stood up, waving to him.

"Here I am!" she called in Spanish. "Are you with Geraldo Huayar?"

The guy stared in shock for a moment. He rushed forward and made a grab at her arm.

She jerked away indignantly. "Hey! Take your hands off of me. I asked you a question. Are you Huayar's man?" she demanded.

"Uhh, yes," the guy answered, startled.

"Then take me to him right away. Some idiot bandits are out here chasing me around. We need to get to Huayar's camp right away where we'll be safe." She commenced dragging him in the opposite direction from the camp.

"Where are you going, lady? The camp's this way."

She gave him her best surprised look. "Really? No wonder I couldn't find it." She let a complaining tone creep into her voice. "I've been wandering around out here in this godforsaken jungle all day trying to find him. You'd think if he wanted me to visit him he'd have given me better directions than just some latitude and longitude coordinates."

"Uhh, right. This way." Her captor took the lead, falling easily into the role of guide to her.

Perfect. No way did she want to enter Huayar's turf dragged in by his men like some helpless prize. She was walking in, head held high, free and on her own terms. It was a small victory, but every win would count against her adversary.

Light began to flicker between the trees. Shouting voices converged around her. Two dozen bandits all toting rifles emerged from the woods as word spread that she'd been found.

The trees gave way to a clearing ringed by shacks in various stages of disrepair. A bonfire burned in the center of the space, and a bloody, battered man lay by it, his arms tied behind his back. She couldn't make out his features clearly, but he was small and wiry and dark-skinned…thank God… not John or Mike or her dad. The man pacing, lionlike, on the far side of the fire caught and riveted her attention. How could that be anyone but Huayar himself?

Rage and power rolled off the man in waves that seemed to bodily hold his people back from him. Or maybe they were just scared of the bastard. *Show no fear. Show no fear….*

All of a sudden, the bandits crisscrossing the woods around John reversed direction like a school of fish darting away from a predator. They turned as one and streamed back toward Huayar's camp.

Hell. They'd captured Melina.

Terror blossomed in his chest, and a desperate need to leap up and save her all but gave away his position to the last of Huayar's men. A steady stream of curses flowed through his mind, and he beat back the litany by force of will, grinding his brain into gear in spite of the panic choking it.

He couldn't rush after her. Huayar's trap had caught one of his prizes, but not both of them. If Melina was to have any chance at all of surviving, he had to remain out here. To bide his time. Wait for his chance. It was their only hope.

Using every trick of stealthy movement he'd ever learned, he eased back toward Huayar's camp. He had to see what was going on, get the lay of the land, look for further traps. It took him only a few minutes to work his way to the edge of the trees where they dissolved into the limestone face of the cliff behind the camp. He peered out from behind the trunk of a massive fir tree at the scene below.

A groan rose in the back of his throat and he only barely managed to prevent it from escaping his lips.

"You're late," Huayar growled.

"You give lousy directions," Melina retorted.

The bandit's head jerked in what looked like equal parts offense and surprise. He studied her more closely. "Where's your soldier boy? He should have been able to bring you right to me."

She shrugged. "I got rid of him after the last village. He didn't want to hike in here on foot. Told me it was too dangerous. So I told him to get lost."

Huayar's intelligent gaze drilled into her, measuring the truth of her words. She crossed her arms and assumed a waiting stance. John had warned her not to be rude or belligerent with the guy, and she schooled her face not to show her thoughts. He strolled over to the bloody man lying on the ground and kicked him viciously in the kidneys. The guy didn't flinch. Unconscious. "Take this sack of garbage out in the woods and shoot him. Nobody steals from me."

Two of Huayar's men ran forward and grabbed the bound man by his armpits. Every fiber in her being screamed for her to beg for the man's life, to do *something* to save the guy. But there was nothing she could do. Huayar held all the cards. All she had going for her were her wits and the desperate hope that John could figure out some way to help her and her family against these overwhelming odds.

Where are you, John? She prayed silently that he was safe and well away from this fiasco. But somehow, she didn't think that was the case.

She started as Huayar's voice cut across her thoughts harshly. "So, you are here now. You will show my men how to make this new drug you have invented."

"Look. I've tried to tell you people over and over that the formula is not perfected. It's not anywhere near refined enough for human consumption. It will take months of lab work to finalize the recipe."

"You will tell me the formula now. My people will do any necessary refining."

Yeah, she'd bet. They would randomly screw around with the mixture until they found one that didn't immediately kill the victims they tried it on and would call it good. How many people would die before they stumbled on the right mix of ingredients? A dozen? A hundred? A thousand, maybe?

"That's not the deal we made. My family goes free. They walk out of here and I receive confirmation that they are back home safe and sound before I tell you a thing."

Huayar's hand flashed out. He slapped her viciously across the face almost before she saw it coming. Her cheek exploded in fiery pain and her neck ached from the unexpected snap of her head to the side. Ohgod, ohgod. *Show no fear.*

She straightened, checking her teeth on that side with her tongue to see if any were loose. She tasted blood. "Slapping me around does nothing to endear me to you, Geraldo. If we're going to be colleagues, we're going to have to establish some ground rules, here."

"Coll—" Huayar broke off, obviously startled. He glared at her as if he wanted to rip her skin back and peer directly into her brain.

She did her damnedest not to give away a thing beneath the intensity of his scrutiny. "That's right. Colleagues." Time to drop a whopper on the guy and shake him up a little. "You don't seriously think you're the only person who's approached me with some sort of business proposition, do you? I studied the market and analyzed you and your competitors long before you resorted to a sophomoric stunt like kidnapping my family."

Jaws dropped all around the fire. Huayar looked skeptical, but rattled. Definitely rattled.

"I had narrowed it down to you and one other…corporate entity…already."

"Who was the other?"

She gave him the name of one of Colombia's most notorious drug lords. The only reason she knew the man's name at all was because she'd heard it dropped at a security meeting within her pharmaceutical firm as someone who would kill to get the formula she was developing. Too bad the same security meeting hadn't included implementation of protective measures for her family. If it had, none of them would be in this pickle now.

Huayar's eyes narrowed in hatred. He must know the drug lord she'd named.

"I will have the formula from you. Now."

She answered evenly. "You will have the formula when my family is out of here. And it's not like you can't continue to use them for collateral against my continued cooperation. Your people can kill them just as easily in Mexico City as they can here."

Huayar actually seemed to consider that. He paced back and forth on the far side of the fire for several minutes.

A gunshot rang out in the woods. She jumped about a foot in the air, then said a silent prayer for the soul of the nameless man. At least he wasn't in any more pain. Perhaps death wasn't the worst fate out here.

Thank goodness she'd talked John out of handing himself over to Huayar to be tortured to death. The thought of having to endure John being mutilated, to hear him screaming in pain like that…nope. She wouldn't have been able to do it. She cared for him far too much for that.

"I need a show of good faith. Give me the list of ingredients for this new drug you have designed."

Her attention swung back to Huayar. Score two points for the guy. He was capable of being reasonable. She weighed how far she dared push him. "Do you have a chemist here?"

"You said the ingredients were readily available. Over the counter."

"They are. But several of them, if handled improperly, could blow this place into last week."

He frowned. But if the guy manufactured methamphetamine, and from the smell of the place he did, then he had a rich appreciation for the dangers of exothermic chemical reactions. Finally, Huayar bellowed, "Get Vito. Bring him here."

She waited tensely while the resident chemist was fetched. Vito turned out to look as Italian as his name sounded, with thick black hair, heavy eyebrows, and a burly frame. He nodded cautiously at Huayar and glanced over at her incuriously. Was that the future awaiting her? Serving at the whim of a madman and doing her best imitation of a robot so as not to draw his random and cruel wrath?

"Tell him," Huayar ordered.

"Do you have some paper? I'll have to write it down. It's a rather lengthy list."

A grimy notebook and a pen were duly passed to her. She scribbled hastily, leaving out several key ingredients. Unlike methamphetamine, which was a relatively simple formula, the one she'd devised involved nearly a dozen steps and twice that many chemicals. But the premise of her work was to only use readily available ingredients, and most of the obvious ones for concocting a drug had already been controlled, to some degree, by governments and industry.

She tore the page out and held it out to Huayar. He gestured at the chemist and she passed the page to Vito. He read down the list carefully. After maybe a minute, he looked up at Huayar. "Not the list. These chemicals cannot form what we seek."

She opened her mouth to protest, but before she could utter a word, Huayar's fist coldcocked her squarely in the jaw. She went down like a rock. The blow didn't knock her out, but the pain was so excruciating that her legs buckled right out from underneath her.

White spots danced in front of her blurry gaze, and she definitely had a couple loose teeth now. Whether she willed it or not, terror exploded inside her. Her ploy hadn't worked.

Huayar was going to torture her and kill her family. She'd failed them all.

"You stupid bitch," a voice snarled above her. A foot slammed into her gut. Already half curled into a fetal position, the kick tightened her into a little ball, just like a roly-poly bug. Except in infinitely more pain, of course. She coughed violently, surprised she hadn't thrown up, too.

In the face of her pain and terror, something odd happened. It was like a switch flipped on in her head. An odd purity of thought came over her, a suspension of time wherein her mind worked at double or triple normal speed, and the events around her seemed to be unfolding in super-slow motion. She watched in detached interest as Huayar drew back to kick her again.

John jumped violently as Huayar's fist smashed into Melina's face. Son of a bitch! No matter that he'd seen people get hit before—hell, he'd slugged people like that himself a few times—he completely lost his composure this time. That was Melina down there! Sweet, gentle Melina, who would never harm a hair on anybody's head.

Whatever they were saying—he couldn't hear their conversation from up here—she'd obviously said something that severely pissed off Huayar. What was on that piece of paper she'd scribbled on, anyway? Surely she hadn't handed over the formula. She, of all people, knew how crucial it was to keep that information out of Huayar's hands. Although, given the swing the bastard had just taken at her, John had to believe that she hadn't given the bandit what he'd wanted.

Hang in there, baby. Don't buckle.

He had to do something fast to save her. She couldn't take too many more blows like that. No way would he let Huayar beat her to death while he sat up here and watched the show. *A diversion.* Maybe he could draw off Huayar and his men.

Except Huayar hadn't left the camp earlier when Melina had been spotted. He'd sent his flunkies out to hunt her down.

Huayar hauled off and kicked Melina in the stomach, and the pain of the blow shot through John's gut as sharply as if the blow had landed on him. He swore under his breath. He saw Melina gasping for air, the breath knocked out of her. Damned if he couldn't make out the tears streaming down her face, too.

In the midst of his panic, an unpleasant truth broke across his disjointed thoughts. Huayar had no reason to hit Melina. She had something he wanted badly. Roughing her up would do nothing to endear her to the bandit. And if Huayar was only trying to make her talk, even the Peruvian knew the fastest way to break her would be to pull out one of her loved ones and make them scream. Why the punching bag act then?

The answer all but hit him over the head.

This little boxing exhibition from Huayar was for John's benefit. The bastard knew he was still out here. After laying eyes on beautiful, vulnerable, gentle Mel, Huayar had reasoned, correctly, that John had to feel plenty protective of her by now, after spending a few days tromping around in the woods with her. Huayar had also figured out that the fastest way to draw out her soldier/guide was to brutally beat her in plain sight.

John swore under his breath.

Huayar wasn't going to let up on Mel until John walked out of these woods and handed himself over.

Huayar's foot drew back again.

And John broke.

He couldn't do it. He couldn't sit up here and do nothing while Melina took this pain meant for him. Plan B was back on the table. He was going down there and handing himself over to Huayar as a hostage in place of Melina's family.

Peace came over him. He would die, but it would be okay. He had let go of his guilt over Afghanistan, or at least arrived at a truce with it. He'd known the love of a good woman. He would be dying for a good cause. Yeah. It would be okay.

Purposefully, he stood up. He shed his gear. Took a step forward.

And slammed to the ground face-first as something impossibly heavy and fast moving smashed into him from behind.

Chapter 16

Melina gathered her courage and lifted her hand away from her face, which was already beginning to swell. She glared up at Huayar and forced herself not to flinch as the bastard wound up to kick her again.

"What kind of idiot do you take me for?" she snapped up at him. "Did you seriously think I was just going to hand over the ingredient list to you? Hit me again and you can forget getting the formula out of me. It'll go to the Colombians and you can go to hell."

His foot stopped at the apex of its backswing. Lowered to the ground. His fist flashed down. She flinched reflexively—she couldn't help it. But instead of plowing into her face again, Huayar grabbed her shirt and hauled her roughly to her feet.

"You're tougher than you look, little girl."

Was that actually a hint of grudging admiration in his voice? She couldn't believe she'd managed to deliver that ultimatum without breaking down in sobs of abject terror.

"I want to see my family. Now."

"No."

"Then you might as well start kicking me again. Because I'm not playing ball with you. The Colombians win."

"What the hell are you talking about, you loco bitch? I could kill you right now."

She shrugged, the movement making her ribs feel like stalks of celery that had been cracked in two. She put aside the pain—she didn't have time for it right now. Her blood adrenaline levels must be off the charts.

She looked right into Huayar's eyes. "Kill me and not only do you not get the formula, but you hand it to your enemies. I've put a copy of the recipe in a safe deposit box in Bogota. If I do not call the bank periodically to report in, the contents of that box will be delivered by bonded courier to your competition."

The back of Huayar's hand lifted, and she stepped forward as if to walk into the blow. "Go ahead. Hit me. Do it, and we're through."

"Your family will die."

"They're dead anyway. You're going to kill them no matter what happens with me."

That made the Peruvian pull back sharply, staring at her assessingly. Didn't expect her to call his hand, did he? The recklessness that had roared through her when she lay on the ground about to be beaten to death faltered. Maybe she shouldn't have brought up the idea so casually of him offing her family. Best to keep that thought out of his head.

Backtracking quickly from her mistake, she took a significantly more conciliatory tone of voice. "Look, Geraldo. I came here to work with you. I expected that our initial negotiation might be fraught with certain misunderstandings. I'm willing to forgive and forget all that's happened tonight. Send my family back home, and I'll gladly hand over the entire formula. Vito and I can work together to tweak it, and you'll get rich beyond imagining when you introduce the synthetic drug of the twenty-first century to the world."

Huayar stared at her.

It took every ounce of willpower she had to keep the expression on her face pleasant and open as she waited for his answer. After all, *everything* depended on the guy swallowing the bait of her offer.

A male voice breathed in John's ear, "What in the hell are you doing, man? You can't walk in there by yourself and get her out!"

Shock rendered John completely speechless for several seconds. The weight rolled off of him, and he looked over at the familiar face of Brady Hathaway. His boss. Out here in the middle of Nowheresville, Peru.

"How— What— I thought you were out on a search-and-rescue!"

"I am. You're the S&R."

"I'm not lost," John replied, stymied.

"The way I heard it, you were."

"Jeez. You mean the noose back at Pirate Pete's? I'm over that. Mel talked me out of killing myself."

Speaking of Melina, John's attention turned back to the scene playing out below. He stared, stunned. She was back on her feet and talking to Huayar again. How in the world had she pulled that off?

"I dunno," Brady replied. "Looked to me like you were planning to march down there and get yourself killed."

"He was hitting her."

Brady's eyebrow cocked. "And you've never seen a girl get hit before?"

"But…it's Mel…."

"Ahh." His boss packed a world of understanding into that single syllable. Comprehension that John had a more than strictly professional interest in her. Much more, dammit.

John closed his eyes in chagrin. Then he spoke urgently. "She's a doctor and a chemist. She's invented a formula for a new drug to replace meth. Huayar kidnapped her family to force her to give the recipe to him. We've got to get her out before she talks."

"Her family still alive?"

"They were as of last night. Mother and father in their late sixties, younger brother in his mid-twenties. In good health and fully mobile."

"Ahh yes, the wannabe drug dealer. And general screwup, Michael. We have quite a file on him."

As he'd thought. The brother was the leak of Melina's research to Huayar. He'd wring the kid's neck when he caught up with him—

"Where are the hostages?" Hathaway asked, interrupting his furious train of thought.

"They were in that third building on the right yesterday, but they weren't there when I took a peek an hour ago. I don't know where they are now. I'd guess Huayar's quarters on the left—that partially buried structure—or the meth lab on the far right."

Hathaway asked sharply, "You've been down in the camp?"

"Yeah."

"I'd ask if you have a death wish, but I already know the answer to that one. That place is way too active for operatives to penetrate safely."

"I've been working outside the usual boundaries of safety a bit on this trip."

Brady snorted. "We noticed. You've been a bear to track, dude."

"We?" John asked hopefully. "Who's here with you?"

"Bravo Squad."

"All of it?" If so, that would mean a dozen Special Forces operatives were here, within striking range of Huayar and his men.

"All of it. Plus a few men from Charlie Squad, and Scottie, Stoner and Ripper from your Alpha Squad. Turns out you're a popular guy. When the Scooby gang heard I was going to try to save you from yourself, I couldn't stop them all from coming. It's a bloody convention out here."

"Hot damn," John murmured in fervent relief.

Brady turned his attention to the camp below. "From the look of it, this still isn't gonna be a walk in the park. Huayar's got at least a hundred troops down there, and those are his elite guard. They're tough, smart and armed to the teeth. Some of those guys are ex-Special Forces. Peruvian Army types. We trained them a few years back. They won't be pushovers."

John nodded, his exuberant relief tempered by the reality of the dangers still before them. But at least there was hope now. Plan B could go back onto the back burner for the moment. "Have you got any spare weapons I could lay my hands on?"

"I think we might be able to scare up a grenade launcher or two for you."

John grinned over at his boss. "In case I haven't mentioned it yet, damn, I'm glad to see you."

"Likewise, old man. Likewise."

Melina followed Huayar's man across the camp to a building whose side walls were partially buried in mounds of dirt. She paused just inside, allowing her eyes to adjust to the dim light of a kerosene lamp sitting on a table off to one side of a narrow central room. After the bright campfire, it took a few seconds to see anything except darkness and that tiny flame of light.

Three shadows stepped away from the wall and materialized into armed, grim-looking men. She pulled back from the threat on their faces.

"What's she doing here?" one of them growled over her shoulder at the guard behind her.

"The boss says to let her see the prisoners."

The questioner nodded silently and jerked his head toward the back of the room. The first guard nodded and prodded her in the back with the tip of his rifle. Her head whipped around, and she glared at the guy until he actually took a step back from her. Score one for the weak little lady whom the men talked over as if she wasn't there.

Prod-free, she headed for the closed door the guards indicated. They went back to lounging around the shadowed walls from whence they'd emerged. Creepy bunch.

As she reached the door, one of the guards stepped forward and inserted a key in a padlock holding the door firmly shut. It rattled loudly, and she heard shuffling noises from the other side. The panel swung open. The guard stared at her impassively, neither giving her permission to enter, nor preventing her.

Abrupt indecision filled her. She eyed that padlock. This could so easily be a trap. Tell the American chick she can see her family, and then lock her up with them. She'd be as helpless as her parents and brother. Although ultimately she was already Huayar's prisoner. Lock or no lock, she couldn't exactly stroll out of this camp and live more than a few minutes or hours. The ease with which Huayar's men had found her before was clear proof of that.

She shrugged and stepped through the door.

"Melina!"

She rushed forward, embracing her mother almost as fiercely as her mother embraced her.

"What in the world are you doing here, child?" Her mother's hands roamed over her face frantically, reassuring herself that Melina was really standing there in the flesh. Her father wrapped his arms around both of them, saying nothing, but clearly no less delighted to see her in his own quiet way. Her mother exclaimed, "Don't tell me these men kidnapped you, too!"

"Not exactly, Mom. How are you? How are all of you?"

Her brother hung back in the shadows a moment longer, but then pasted on a smile and stepped forward. "Hey, Sis."

"Hey, Mike. How are you?"

"Okay."

He sounded cautious. Wary, even. She asked, "Have they hurt you? Fed you all right?"

Her brother shrugged. "It isn't exactly the Ritz, but they haven't treated us too badly."

Her mother fussed over her, running her hands down Melina's arms and squeezing her hands almost compulsively. "These boys have been polite, all things considered. They have a hard life out here. The Peruvian government has been hard on them."

She snorted. Apparently, no one had told her mom what Huayar and his men did for a living. Just as well. No need to completely terrify the woman. She glanced over at her father. "How's your heart holding up, dad? Any chest pains?" He'd had a mild heart attack a few years back, but had not had any recurrences. So far. The stress of being the prisoner of a vicious killer could do him in fast enough.

"I'm fine, honey. Ready to get out of here."

She smiled gamely at him. "I'm working on it, Dad."

Michael piped up. "What was all that hollering earlier? They told us they caught a bandit trying to rob them."

She opened her mouth to tell the truth, but then glanced down at her mother's naïvely blank face. No need to elaborate on the gory details. It would only upset her parents needlessly. She made eye contact with her brother, though, and they traded significant looks. His eyes darkened with comprehension. Fear followed closely on its heels in his black gaze. At least he understood the gravity of their situation.

"Have you come to take us home, honey?" her mother asked.

"I don't think I'll be going with you, but yes, I think Huayar is prepared to let you go."

She caught a small movement out of the corner of her eye. Her brother had flinched. Dawning suspicion quickly turned into horror as she gazed across the room at him. Under the weight of her steady stare, guilt gradually bowed his shoulders. She was in front of him in two strides and had him by the shirt.

"You told, didn't you?" she accused.

"I—uhh—"

"Melina! Turn your brother loose. We don't act like that in this family!"

She reacted out of reflex to her mother's berating tone and let Mike go. She took a step forward, though, and got right in her brother's face. Under her breath so only he could hear, she snarled, "You told, didn't you?"

"They were going to kill me, Sis. I had nothing else."

"Why? How'd you get mixed up with people like this?"

"I needed cash. I just carried some stuff around. No big deal."

"You were a mule for Huayar? You moved his drugs for him?" she demanded in disbelief.

Mike didn't answer, but he didn't need to. The answer swam miserably in his eyes.

"What the hell were you thinking? Didn't you think about Mom and Dad? About me?"

"I told you. I needed the money. It was quick and easy. Pick up a package, drive it across the border into the States. Drop it off. Two grand for two days' work."

"Jeez, Mike. You could've asked me for a loan if you were that hard up. Look at the mess we're all in now."

His face crumpled. "I screwed up. Bad. We're all gonna die, aren't we?"

He sounded on the verge of tears. She was angry enough at him to take a certain satisfaction in his remorse, but a kernel of love for her idiot brother—buried very deep at the moment—stilled her tongue from any further recriminations.

"I'm doing my darnedest to get us all out of this thing alive.

I need your help. Do what I tell you to and go along with anything I say, okay?"

"Do you have a plan?" Mike asked eagerly. "What is it?"

She glanced at the walls unsure if Huayar's men could hear them or not. "Just go with the flow, okay?"

He nodded, a pitifully hopeful look in his eyes.

She murmured, "I'm not going to get to leave with you guys. I'll need you to lead Mom and Dad out of here. I've got maps. Supplies. Some contacts for you. Can you at least handle that without screwing it up?"

He nodded eagerly, grasping at the flimsy straw of redemption she'd held out before him.

She sighed, not at all sure he could pull it off. After spending the past week with a man like John Hollister, she understood just how immature and incompetent Mike really was by comparison. John she would trust with all their lives. Mike? Not so much.

The door opened and her guide stuck his head in. "Time to go. You owe the boss a recipe."

Mike's gaze snapped to hers in dismay. "You're handing it over?"

"What the hell other choice did you leave me, little brother?" she snapped at him. And with that, she turned on her heel and stalked from the room. She didn't look back. She couldn't. She'd lose it if she did. Her relief at seeing her parents safe and sound and her disappointment in her brother were almost more than she could bear. She wanted to sit down in the middle of the floor and cry her head off. Not yet. Not until they were out of here, away from Huayar and his fists and his hired guns.

Walking into the middle of an operational Special Forces hide with so many familiar faces around him, their movements and equipment as natural to him as breathing, was disconcerting. John had been roaming around out here with little more than camping gear for so long, it felt weird to strap on a utility belt and a headset and a submachine gun. It was like coming back to the land of the living after wandering in some alien landscape for a very long time.

Sadness hovered close to the surface of his soul. The last time he'd been out in the field like this, he'd been with his guys. His team. Oh, a few of the old Alpha Squad faces were here—Scotty and Stoner and Ripper—but so many more were missing.

He'd known guys before who'd died. It was inevitable in their line of work. But to lose so many at once, to carry the memory of their bloodied bodies and empty eyes, that was hard.

"You okay?" Hathaway murmured from behind him.

"No, I'm not okay."

Hathaway nodded soberly. "That may be the healthiest thing I've heard you say since you got back from Afghanistan."

John managed a reasonably casual shrug.

Hathaway looked down at the ground. Back up at John. "I've lost some men on my watch. There's no explaining what that feels like to someone who hasn't experienced it. It's a knife that cuts all the way through you, but doesn't quite kill you. It leaves you hurting so bad you wish you were dead, but instead you just suffer."

John nodded wearily. Oh, how he knew the feeling.

Hathaway continued, "The shrinks would probably tell me to b.s. you and say it gets better. But it doesn't. You just learn to live with it, and after a while, the pain dulls enough to stand. It sucks."

For some reason, hearing rock solid Brady Hathaway admitting to the same weakness he'd been laboring under helped. John looked his boss squarely in the eye. "Thanks." No need to explain what for. They both knew.

Hathaway nodded. After a moment of silence, he smiled grimly. "Ready to go kick us some bad guy ass?"

John smiled back, actually feeling a faint glow of the old passion he'd once carried for his job. "Let's do it."

Melina smelled the meth lab before she saw it. At least Huayar'd had the good sense to set the building a little ways away from the others. Meth manufacturing was a notoriously touchy process. Even with a knowledgeable chemist like Vito around, meth labs had an unfortunate tendency to blow up without warning.

Not surprisingly, the guard stopped well shy of the entrance to the lab and gestured for her to go in alone. She nodded and entered the building.

The crackle of a spotter's voice came over John's headset. "We've got a problem. One of our friendlies just entered the lab. The young woman."

John swore under his breath. Huayar was wasting no time putting Mel to work reproducing the synthetic drug formula for him.

Hathaway nodded tersely, and without missing a beat said, "Change in plans. Cowboy, it looks like you get to sneak into camp and rescue the damsel in distress after all."

John nodded grimly. "When do I go?" If he were in charge, he'd send himself down to infiltrate the camp after staging some sort of minor diversion elsewhere. Nothing big enough to alarm folks, but enough to cause everyone's attention to be elsewhere for a few minutes.

Hathaway turned away. "Scotty, when you wire the water tower, can you cause one of the legs to partially buckle without collapsing, and then wire a second charge to bring it down separately so it looks more like a natural collapse?"

The demolitions man nodded. "No sweat. I had a look at it a few minutes ago. Pretty flimsy construction. Very small charges will work. Minimal noise or flash."

Scotty, Stoner and Ripper had still been in the Middle East debriefing a civilian woman who'd helped them nab a notorious terrorist last fall when John had gotten the call to take the rest of the team over to Afghanistan. To die, as it turned out. Pure luck had saved the three of them from the same fate that had met the rest of their team. Memory of the carnage threatened to surface again.

John forced the images away. Now was not the time to indulge in agonizing flashbacks. Mel was counting on him.

Hathaway came up over John's headset. "Everyone say status. Final checkoff before we move."

Which was to say, this was everyone's last chance to add any information to the battle plan that might cause it to be tweaked. The checkoff went quickly, and no one had anything to add or clarify. They all knew what they were supposed to do. The plan called for a combination of stealth, diversion and positioning for a frontal assault, should it become necessary.

At the end of the roll call, Hathaway said, "Time hack on my count. The time is ten forty-two local time in…three…two…one…hack."

John's watch was two seconds fast. He made a note of the disparity to make corrections as needed later, and said a silent prayer that this night's work would not come down to two-second anythings.

Hathaway said briskly, "Let's move out, men."

Chapter 17

Melina looked up from the worktable in the lab at the pesky guard. "What do you mean, come with you? I'm not going anywhere! I've barely had time to look at this facility, let alone check if the equipment I'll need is here."

Huayar's man shrugged and gestured more insistently for her to come along. She was really getting tired of being treated like a dog.

She said more forcefully, "I have work to do if Huayar wants me to make his drug for him."

"Change of plans," the guy growled.

"What change?" she demanded. "I want to talk to Huayar. Right now. I appreciate that he's used to being in charge, but if he and I are going to work together, he's got to keep me in the loop. He can start getting used to that right now."

"Fine. He said to bring you to his quarters anyway. You can talk to him when we get there."

She subsided, a little sheepish after her big speech. Without further protest, she followed him toward one of the more solid-looking sleeping huts. "I thought he lived in that building over there." She pointed at the building John had identified as Huayar's headquarters, the one where she'd visited her family.

"Nah. That's the ammo dump."

Ammo dump? Uh oh. John was out there sneaking around the woods, no doubt planning to stage some dramatic rescue of her, and he'd told her earlier that Huayar would probably keep her close to himself—*in that building*. John would head straight for the ammo dump, and those creepy guys lurking in its shadows. He would be walking right into a giant trap.

She wanted to shout a warning up at the trees and the man they hid, but she dared not. If he was going to save her family, she couldn't in any way give away his presence out there. She had to keep up the charade that she'd parted ways with him.

For the moment, she had arrived at a truce with Huayar, and as long as he thought she was here alone, and ultimately at his mercy, he would remain confident that she'd eventually cough up the formula. Thankfully, he was willing to play nice for now. Well, relatively nice. She reached up absently to rub her aching jaw. But who knew how long that would hold up. She had to get her family away from this monster.

Get my family, John. Leave me and get my family.

"Snipers, report." Hathaway ordered over the radio.

John listened in as the four shooters reported being in position around the camp and eyes-on-target. They were going to play hell with any kind of armed response Huayar tried to mount to their infiltration. There was something supremely demoralizing, not to mention chaos-causing, about death raining down from points unknown. He should know. He'd been the fish in a barrel before, and as Brady had so succinctly put it, it sucked.

Hathaway made a series of complicated clicks over the radio, signaling him and the other rescue team to move in on the camp. John would come in from the south and try to snag Melina, since he recognized her on sight and more importantly, she recognized him on sight. Four other men would make for Mel's family and try to sneak them out of the camp. And just in case it all went to hell, the rest of Hathaway's men would position themselves for a firefight.

John gripped his weapon tightly, startled to realize his palms were sweating. The thought of being caught out in the middle of another gun battle made his skin crawl. He and Melina seriously needed to clear the camp's perimeter before any bullets starting flying.

Brady had mentioned that the Peruvian government had not okayed a military action on its soil, which was diplomatic speak for Hathaway and company weren't supposed to get into a shootout with Huayar. No surprise. The drug lord must have a ton of Peruvian politicians in his pocket to have survived this long. Not only would they be well-paid to protect him, but they also wouldn't be thrilled to have their source of extracurricular income cut off if Huayar was killed.

However, Uncle Sam wasn't going to shed a tear over any stray bullets that happened to fly in Huayar's direction. Hathaway had deployed his troops in anticipation of a major shooting engagement, and John was frankly going to be surprised if it didn't come to one. But in the meantime, he was praying the stealth approach to finding and freeing Melina and her family would work. Once lead started flying, the odds of innocents dying went up astronomically.

Hathaway hadn't initially wanted to send him in on this extraction. He said John was too close to Melina, still healing from his ordeal. Nice turn of phrase. Healing. Maybe he'd quit bleeding, but that hardly constituted healing. He'd argued with Hathaway that Melina would be least likely to freak out and give away the op if he materialized in front of her without warning instead of one of the other guys. When that hadn't swayed Brady, he'd resorted to begging. It hadn't been pretty. But the boss-man had relented. Thank God. He'd be damned if he was going to sit on the sidelines chewing his fingernails while Bravo Squad went and got his girl.

He'd forecasted to Hathaway that she'd refuse to leave until her family went, too. As a result, Hathaway had adjusted the timetable to give the other rescue team a head start. John wouldn't move in to grab her until the first team was nearly finished with its task.

Hathaway clicked the command for Rescue Team One to move at will. John couldn't see them, but they'd be leapfrogging their way from hiding spot to hiding spot right now, working their way down the same heavily forested slope he'd descended earlier. One of Bravo Squad's spotters had been continuously watching the earth-bermed building Melina had gone into and left earlier, and so far, no other hostages had come out of the structure.

John and Hathaway had reasoned that she'd refuse to do anything for Huayar until she saw her family. Given that it was the first building she'd been taken to after Huayar initially smacked her around, and she'd only stayed inside about five minutes, he and Hathaway shared a high level of confidence that it was where her family was being held.

It figured. The hostages always were located in the most inconvenient spot for a rescue. They couldn't be out in one of the nice, flimsy sleeping shacks. Nope. Had to be holed up in the lone building built liked a damned ammo bunker.

He crested the last ridge and caught a glimpse of flickering light through the trees. Huayar's camp. He crouched, making his way cautiously toward the south end of the camp. A cluster of sleeping shacks lay between him and the meth lab, whose stink was acrid in his nose. He glanced at his watch. Once he was in place, he'd have about thirty endless minutes to sit, cooling his jets while the other rescue team did its thing. Of course, the wait would give him time to get the feel of this end of the camp, to find the flow of its movements, maybe even to spot Melina.

I'm coming, baby. Just a little while longer.

Melina ducked inside the dirt-floored shack, its walls a crazed hodgepodge of plywood, random lumber and galvanized tin. A half-dozen hammocks hung around the margins of the room, but the center of the space was open, filled at the moment by a folding table and a cluster of men looking at something on top of it. She edged a little farther into the room, trying to catch a glimpse of what they were all studying so intently.

A crudely sketched map. Based on the maps John had made her memorize earlier, she recognized the terrain. It was the valley holding this camp.

"...probably come over this ridge...don't know who this bastard is, but let's assume he's a one-man army."

"...handled himself like a military type...had a bag of weapons in his vehicle..."

Melina jolted. These guys had searched the Land Rover? When? Must've been during that interminable afternoon she and John had spent sitting in that cantina waiting for the real muscle of Huayar's outfit to arrive. But then the import of what she was hearing slammed into her. Huayar and his men were expecting John to come after her, and they were laying a massive ambush for him.

Fingers of cold dread clutched at her. Oh, no. Not another ambush. He would fall apart for sure this time. He was only just now beginning to recover from the last one. If anyone else he cared about died in another ill-fated gun battle, John would self-destruct right there, on the spot. Not to mention the fact that she'd undoubtedly die, too, and with her, any hope for her family's escape alive from this nightmare.

She stood with her back to the wall, as still and silent as a mouse, in hopes that Huayar wouldn't notice her presence. She had no idea if or how she could help John, but the more she knew about his enemy's plan, the better. As she listened to Huayar deploying his men in and around the camp in a series of hidden, concentric rings, her last, lingering hopes faded. John could never succeed against this many men, particularly if they were all out there waiting and watching for him.

After an eternity, the minute hand on John's watch finally passed the thirty-minute mark. His usual patience stretched to its limit, he was immensely relieved simply to move again. He'd picked out his approach about twenty-nine minutes ago, and now he commenced the slow trip down to the camp's perimeter. His path took him through the gap between a pair of guards who were busily staring outward into the deep jungle. Poor guys had no idea he was parked only about thirty feet from them. Their loss.

That thirty feet took him a good ten minutes to creep until he reached the edge of the camp. The bad news was that Huayar obviously expected trouble tonight. He had patrol teams roaming the entire camp. The good news was they'd been at it long enough to have settled into routine routes walked at predictable paces. It was an easy thing to slip past them.

He wondered briefly how Rescue Team One was doing, but then pushed the thought from his mind. Not his job. They'd do their mission, he'd do his. Momentary satisfaction flowed through him at the well-oiled machine Bravo Squad was. It dawned on him that he'd missed this seamless teamwork, the sense of doing the impossible with ease; hell, of having a goal. Any goal. He'd been drifting along for so long doing nothing. He'd forgotten what having a purpose felt like.

Hathaway sent a single click across the radios. First check-in. Everyone gave a single click response back to indicate their progress one hour into the plan. The other rescue team was supposed to have located the hostages and be near them, ready to commence the actual extraction. They clicked once, and he breathed a sigh of relief.

When his turn in the rotation came up, he gave the single click back to indicate he was on or ahead of schedule—meaning he'd made it into the camp proper.

The check-in finished. No double clicks came back. Perfect. As a commander, he always expected glitches in the plan, and was pleasantly surprised when none popped up. So far, so good.

Just before he'd headed out this way, one of the spotters had reported that Melina had gone into the sleeping shack nearest to the meth lab. Nobody'd seen her since then, so the assumption was she was still in that structure. Not that he was complaining. It would make pulling her out a far sight easier. He could simply go in through a back wall and sneak her out into the woods. No fuss, no muss. At least that was the plan. It was almost too easy. Wary of another trap, he approached the camp this time with even more caution than before.

Rescue Team One should be working their way in through a back window of the bunker right about now. It was a tricky moment, one where they could easily be spotted. The minutes ticked past as he eased from shadow to shadow, making his way slowly around the camp to his target.

Another check-in at an hour plus thirty. Rescue Team One indicated they had a man inside with the hostages. John's single click indicated that he'd located Melina, was in place near her, awaiting the go-ahead to pull her out.

He heard men's voices inside the shack he believed her to be in, and eased himself upright enough to peer in a crack about a foot above ground level. Holy crap! Huayar! He froze, his brain going a mile a minute. Melina was in here with him? He allowed his gaze to slide left. Six more men who looked like Huayar's senior lieutenants. A couple were positively ex-military, still sporting military haircuts and pieces of their former uniforms.

He looked to the right. There. Across the room. Melina's hiking boots. She was standing in a dark corner, very still. He couldn't see her face from this angle. Her position in the room could be a problem. He pondered ways to lure her over to this side of the building. Not that it would help as long as Huayar and his men were sitting in there with the lights on where they could see her.

He was going to need a diversion. Preferably one that involved knocking out the camp's electricity. And then he was going to need a heaping helping of luck. Failing that, he was going to need speed and surprise to get in there, grab her, and get out before Huayar and company realized what was going on. Problem was, the drug lord and his men were all experienced field operators. They wouldn't panic if the lights went out, and furthermore, they'd quickly and correctly identify a diversion as just that and would tend to stay put right where they were until the dust settled.

He swore under his breath. They might have to resort to the Plan B firefight after all.

Another frustrating half hour passed, and Rescue Team One clicked that it was hung up and unable to egress with the hostages. He clicked that he, too, was unable to proceed. After a brief pause, Hathaway clicked a series of commands that made John's jaw clench grimly. Plan B, indeed. Hathaway was throwing Plan C and Plan D at Huayar, too.

All hell was about to break loose.

It was all Melina could do to stand there in the corner and not tear her hair out. These men were calmly and coolly plotting John's death! She wanted to run out of here screaming to him at the top of her lungs, but instead, she had to stand around looking supremely disinterested. She didn't for a minute think Huayar was actually ignoring her. He was too clever not to be keeping a surreptitious eye on her. He no doubt was gauging her reaction to the entire conversation to see if it got a rise out of her. Hence, the absolute necessity of showing no reaction at all.

She didn't know whether to pray for John to come right away and get her out of here now, or to pray for him to wait until Huayar and his men eventually let their guard down before he tried a rescue. If they ever let their guard down.

A radio crackled in the middle of the table. A tense voice reported movement in the woods on the west side of camp. Abruptly, all eyes in the shack were on Huayar. Except he looked over at her. Melina steeled herself to look back at him as casually as she could.

"Is that your guy?" Huayar snapped.

"How should I know? I left him back at that village. I can't imagine why he'd follow me out here. It's probably a bear, attracted by the smell of food." She added dryly, "Or maybe the bear's a meth addict looking to cop a free hit."

Brief grins greeted her comment, but Huayar's intense stare never wavered. Still studying her with predatory intensity, he ordered, "Julio, take some men and go have a look."

One of the flunkies nodded and stepped outside.

Silence settled over the tent, tense now with waiting. She picked a spot on the wall to study and shifted her weight from foot to foot, her legs growing tired. There were no empty chairs in the room, and she dared not plop down on somebody's hammock without permission.

A muffled bang made everyone in the room look up.

She jumped, both at the odd noise, a hollow *whump*, from outside, and at the way Huayar leaped to his feet, his eyes wild. *What was that noise?* It resonated too deeply for a gunshot, but wasn't loud enough for a bomb. Huayar seemed to know what it was, though, for swearing his head off, he grabbed up a rifle and bolted for the door with his men in tow.

A strange rushing noise erupted outside, along with the sounds of shouting and general chaos. Huayar and his lieutenants vacated the tent completely at that outburst. What in the world?

The naked lightbulb hanging in the center of the room flickered and went out. Unsure of what to do with herself, she stepped away from the wall with the notion of heading for the door. But then a black specter rose up before her out of the ground itself, and her mouth opened on a scream.

Off to his right, John saw the water tower keel over in majestic slow motion, spilling its entire contents in a flood that rushed through the center of the camp a foot deep. He didn't hear the separate charge that took out the camp's main electric generator, but it was timed to coincide with the flood and mimic a shortout. The camp went black as the lights went off, and the big bonfire met its sudden end in the flood. He raised his night vision goggles from around his neck, and the camp leaped out at him in bright relief. Huayar's people scurried every which way like a bunch of agitated ants. Assured that no one was looking this way, he peeled back the plywood panel whose screws he'd already loosened, and slipped into the shack. Melina's familiar profile was just turning toward him.

She lurched, opening her mouth to scream as he lunged forward and wrapped his arms around her, slapping a hand over her mouth. "It's me, Mel."

She sagged in his arms, then threw herself against him, all but choking him as she knocked his NVG's askew.

He whispered, already drawing her toward the hole in the wall, "No time for hugs, baby. We've got to go."

Gunfire erupted outside. Lots of it. Crap. So much for stealth.

"My family—" Melina started.

He cut her off. "Rescue Team One's with them. You and I won't leave the area until they do."

She nodded, her grateful smile looking more like a macabre grimace to him through the goggles.

"Let's get out of here," he muttered. He led the way through the hole, holding the plywood back as she crawled through it. The remnants of the flood were seeping this way, turning the camp's packed dirt into a slippery morass.

She made a noise of disgust, and he cautioned under his breath, "No noise, baby."

She nodded, picking her way beside him on her hands and knees to the nearest bush. At least it was dry back here. He leaned close to breathe in her ear, "We'll make our way a little farther up the hill and hide there."

She gave him a thumbs-up and he spared a moment to smile down at her. He trailed his fingertips gently down her swollen cheek and then touched her lips. It was the best he could do in the circumstances to communicate everything he felt for her. She leaned into his palm with her tender cheek. That had to hurt, and he lifted his hand away from her.

They turned to head up the hill and he took one last glance over his shoulder behind them to check for signs of pursuit.

He stopped. Swore violently under his breath. He murmured to Melina, "Change of plans."

Chapter 18

Melina turned to look at what had put that ominous tone in John's voice, and gasped. At least fifty of Huayar's men surrounded the bunker. Panic leaped in her gut. Her family! She had to do something! She'd go down there and demand to know what Huayar was up to. John would just have to try to rescue her another time. She started to stand up.

"My parents! Mike—" She broke off as John commenced muttering under his breath, a continuous stream of invectives with a distinct note of panic in it. She dropped back down beside him, a sick feeling of dread heavy inside her. "What's wrong?"

"Ohgodohgodohgod…"

The same litany started up in her head. She was missing something here, and it couldn't possibly bode well for her family. A man like John in complete meltdown was beyond bad. It was disastrous. She just wasn't sure how, yet.

He groaned, "Huayar thinks that's me in there. Oh, God.

They'll be shot like fish in a barrel. My fault. Bastard's after me...."

"I don't understand, John. What's going on?"

"Four guys from Pirate Pete's...in there with your family...they'll all die...."

If it was possible to feel any sicker, she did. Not again. Not more of his comrades ambushed, this time in front of his eyes instead of around him. She squeezed her eyes shut, desperately wishing away this nightmare. But when she opened them again, that deadly ring of muzzle flashes around the building was still flashing in the night.

"Gotta save them," John mumbled.

She grabbed his arm in alarm. "There are dozens of men shooting at that bunker. You can't take them all. Heck, you probably don't even have that many bullets!"

He glanced over at her, and she reeled back from the look in his eyes. It was already dead.

"Not. Happening. Again," he ground out. "Not on my watch."

He sounded like it was all he could do to hold it together. She said quickly, "I'll go with you. Tell me what to do."

"You stay." He swore again and brought his weapon up into a firing position at his right shoulder. He stood up, emerging out of the brush like death rising from the earth itself.

"But I can't lose you too—"

He was gone, racing down the hill, silent and lethal, deliberate flashes from his muzzle charting his course for her toward the ring of fire.

Dismayed, terrified, and torn in two, she crouched in the woods with the smells of dirt and crushed leaves rising around her as Death feasted before her. John was going to die. He was going to charge in there all alone and sacrifice himself in the name of trying to save his friends. This time, there was no way he'd walk out of it alive. He'd make darn sure of that. She'd lost him. His demons had won.

A sob shook her.

It was so damned unfair. She'd finally found the man of her heart, and now she was supposed to sit here and watch him die. If only she knew what to do. If only she had a rifle and could shoot them all, or a missile she could shoot to blow up Huayar and his men—

Her thoughts derailed abruptly. *Blow them up.*

She glanced over at the meth lab not far from her. She was a chemist, for crying out loud. She was the queen of playing with stuff that blew up, and right in front of her was a whole building full of volatile and highly explosive chemicals. She might not manage to destroy the whole camp, but she could create a hell of a diversion for John.

She rose to a half crouch and zigzagged down the hill, dodging trees and brush the same way John had a moment before. She raced into the camp. A man jumped out in front of her, pointing a rifle at her head. She recognized one of Huayar's men from earlier.

"It's me!" she shouted in Spanish over the shooting behind him. "I've got to secure the lab. It could blow with all this gunfire! Let me pass!"

The guy got an alarmed look in his eyes and waved the tip of his rifle at the lab to his left, indicating for her to get moving.

She ran on, grimly ducking at each new burst of gunfire. *Please be alive, John. Just a few more seconds. Don't die on me. Not yet.* She burst through the doorway and into the lab. Deserted. Thank God. The cluttered stacks of barrels, crude cook fires and filthy packing tables were as different from her pristine, stainless steel lab as could be. By the dim flicker of the firelight, she raced around the room, searching frantically for what she'd need. It had to be fast. Simple. A half-dozen ways to combine the many volatile components of methamphetamine into an explosive mix came to her mind, but many of them were multi-step reactions she didn't have time to mess with. She needed a bomb, not a fire.

There. A stack of foot-long metal bottles. Perfect. Propane camp fuel. She ran to one of the big cauldrons hanging over a flame and swung it aside, dumping its liquid contents on the ground. She held her breath as a cloud of noxious fumes rose up. She didn't even want to think about what was in that cloud—vaporized drain cleaner, toluene brake fluid, chloroform—ugh.

Her eyes watering, she swung the now-empty cauldron back over the fire. Quickly, she grabbed an armful of the propane fuel bottles and tossed them into the pot. She added a bucket of red phosphorus, and tossed in a pile of sodium shavings for good measure. It would take a minute or two to heat the bottles sufficiently for one of them to blow. But once it went, the chain reaction would be spectacular.

She glanced around the room. She could enhance the whole thing with some vaporized gases in here, too. Ahh. There. Ether. She ran over to the store of ether tanks and opened all the stopcocks. Like any decent meth lab, this place was well-ventilated to prevent a buildup of explosive gases. Holding her breath as best she could, she raced around the room, closing all the shutters she could reach.

She reached an opening that looked out upon the bunker and the circling mass of Huayar's men. She paused to take in the scene. Where was John? Was he already one of those ominous black heaps of clothing on the ground? Or was he still out there somewhere, fighting for all he was worth to save his buddies? *Please be alive.*

John dodged behind a shack, running low around its far side and double-tapping a pair of bullets into the nearest bandit. A second hostile turned, and John dropped him, too. Gripped in a fugue state of see-and-kill, he roamed the night, shooting everyone who crossed his path. *Must save those men.*

A mountain in Afghanistan flashed before his eyes. *Tap-tap*. Another bandit down. Blood. So damned much blood. He shot another pair of Huayar's men. The screams. He'd never forget his men's dying pleas for help. And there he'd been, shot in the back himself, helpless as a baby. A bandit spun to face him, raising his weapon, startled. John mowed him down with a fusillade of shots. Only long habit with ammunition preservation stopped him from emptying his weapon into the Afghani—no, wait, Peruvian—rebel.

He blinked, disoriented. Where was he? Trees. Greenery. Shouted Spanish commands. *Peru*. He passed a grimy hand across his eyes.

Melina.

As soon as he thought of her, the worst of his flashback drained away, replaced by a sense of calm. He knew what he had to do. If she wouldn't leave until her family did, then he'd just have to free her family for her, even if it meant giving his life to do it. He'd die for her in a second. He looked around, surprised to see how close to the main ring of Huayar's men he'd pushed. He was all but on top of the line.

The majority of Huayar's men hadn't caught on to the fact yet that shots were coming from behind them, in addition to theirs pouring into the bunker. The rescue team inside had yet to fire. They probably were afraid to draw fire to the hostages, not to mention that their current rules of engagement precluded them from starting a gun battle on Peruvian soil.

John eased backward into the deep shadows beside a shack and took stock. He needed better cover if he was going to shoot a hole in this mass of men. All of a sudden, the night and shadows and the muzzle bursts looked just like that other firefight, that other line of hostile shooters unloading on him and his men. Except this time, he was on his feet, his weapon nestled against his shoulder, and the bad guys were in his sights. He wasn't technically part of Hathaway's team, therefore, by his reasoning, he was exempt from the no gunfighting order. Satisfaction surged through him. Payback time.

He took aim, firing deliberately and to kill. He had about two hundred more rounds on him, which should be enough to hold him for another ten to twelve minutes. Plenty of time to eliminate Huayar and his men. But if he had anything to say about it, this whole thing would be over long before then.

"Cowboy, pull back. You're entering our field of fire."

He started at hearing his handle over the radios. It had been a while since anyone used it. Besides, he was in command and gave the orders on this mountain—no wait. Hathaway was here. How did he get out here? Disoriented, John vaguely heard his commander repeat the command. *Whatever.*

Resolutely, he kept on firing.

"Pull back, John. Now." That was Hathaway's clipped voice barking the order at him. He responded reflexively to the whiplash tone in his commander's voice and lowered his weapon. He took a step back.

Hathaway ordered sharply, "Secure your target, Cowboy."

His target. *Melina.* A small measure of sanity seeped back into his consciousness. He was in a valley in Peru in the middle of a shootout. Where was she, anyway? She'd better be back on that hill. Of course, she hadn't stayed put the last time he told her to. What were the odds she'd done as he ordered this time? Crap. He took off running back across the camp. He cleared all around him as he went, keeping an eye out for laggards or cowards in Huayar's ranks, hiding from the fight. After all, a rat's bullet killed just as well as a hero's.

What was that over there? Someone was hiding in the meth lab. A straggler back here could easily spot him and Melina in the woods behind the camp and take one or both of them out. He'd have to clear the building. He sprinted for the lab and its volatile contents.

* * *

Melina ducked under a worktable as a black shape hurtled into the lab. Now what? That cauldron wasn't hot enough to blow quite yet. It needed another minute or two. Huayar's man couldn't find it! She intentionally dodged behind a stack of crates of pseudoephedrine tablets, hoping the guy would see her movement and come investigate.

Sure enough, the intruder spun around the end of the pile, the bore of his rifle leading the way. Prepared to stand up and berate the guy for scaring her, she stared at the big black-clad figure wearing elaborate goggles over his eyes. *Not Huayar's man!* She barely had time to register that before the figure's rifle swung up and away from her. He stepped forward and swept her into his dark grasp.

Only as his head buried itself in her hair did it dawn on her. "John!" she cried. "Thank God, you're alive! My family?"

"They're still alive in there. Huayar's men haven't penetrated the place."

She sagged in relief, her legs all but collapsing out from under her.

Supporting her easily, John continued, "Our guys have enough firepower to hold off Huayar indefinitely in that hole. Assuming there's not a back door."

"A back door?" she repeated, confused.

"Bad guys have a tendency to put secret escape tunnels in any place they think they might get trapped someday. I'm worried that Huayar's got men crawling down some secret tunnel as we speak to breach the place."

She gasped, alarmed afresh. "We have to do something!"

He nodded. "We're hamstrung out here because our rules of engagement prohibit us from launching a major firefight with Huayar."

"What in the heck do you call that?" she gestured outside at the barrage of gunfire.

"That's Huayar firing at our guys, and our guys not returning fire. That's not a gunfight. Trust me. You'll know if we start shooting back."

"To heck with your rules of engagement! Let's assault those guys before they get into the bunker!"

He grinned down at her, a slash of white in the darkness of his face. "You and me? Like Bonnie and Clyde?"

"Why not? I've got a diversion cooking over there." She glanced over at the cauldron where a few sparks were starting to jump. Any second that thing would blow.

"What have you done?" he asked, startled.

"I've cooked up an explosion. Should go any second."

"What's in that pot?"

"A bunch of propane tanks, red phosphorus and sodium shavings. And the ether bottles are open over there."

"Holy sh— We've got to get out of here!"

"We go get my folks and my brother, right?"

"No. We head for the woods and take cover from your apocalyptic brew."

"John, I'm not leaving—"

"You are leaving. *Now*. If I have to carry you!"

He made a grab for her legs and she danced back from him. She glanced over at the cauldron, which was definitely beginning to smoke. The smell of ether was strong in the air, too.

"Honey, there are fifteen commandos out there, waiting for me to get you out of here. They can't do anything until you're secured."

"Commandos? I thought you said they were your buddies...."

"They are. I'll explain outside." He grabbed her upper arm in his powerful grasp, and all but lifted her off the ground as he propelled her from the building. Once outside, her instinct to get away from the lab took over, and she sprinted beside John for the trees.

The flash came first. She and John leaped simultaneously

for a huge, downed tree, landing across it and rolling behind it as a deafening concussion of sound slammed into her. She clapped her hands over her ears as the explosion rocked through the forest. John rolled on top of her, shielding her as debris and tree branches rained down from above for several seconds.

"You okay?" he bit out.

She nodded beneath him, too crushed to make a sound.

He rolled off of her and she popped up beside him to peer at her handiwork. Another explosion sent a fireball up into the night just then, and they ducked behind the log once more.

John shook his head at her in amazement.

She grinned back. "Can I cook, or can I cook?"

Static crackled in John's ear and then Hathaway's voice materialized from the chaotic noise. "Report, Cowboy! What the hell was that?"

He keyed his microphone. "Mel thought we could use a diversion."

"Remind me never to piss her off," Hathaway bit out. "All teams report."

A quick checkoff revealed that everyone had survived the blast, including the team trapped in the bunker, although a couple of their guys had busted eardrums. A moment of silence ensued, and then shouting voices erupted over the radios.

"…incoming fire!"

"Say location!"

"…coming out of the woods…"

"…surrounded…"

John whirled to face the slope behind them, his back against the log. "Get on the other side of the log. Now," he ordered Melina tersely.

She rolled across the broad surface, and as John plunked down beside her, asked him, "What's happening?"

"Ambush. Huayar's got more men out there."

She cast her mind back frantically to the briefing she'd overheard earlier. "Does it mean anything when Huayar said, 'Deploy fire teams one through four on the ridges. On my signal close the net'?"

John stared at her. "Where did you hear that?"

"It's what Huayar told his men earlier."

"How many men does he have?"

"He had about six men around the table with him. I think they each had about twenty-five men."

Crap. He keyed his mike. "Mel says total troop strength is around 150. With the fifty in the camp, we're looking at about a hundred men closing from the ridges in four fire teams."

He didn't need to be standing beside Hathaway to hear the guy swearing under his breath and thinking fast. How in the hell were they supposed to get out of here with a force that size closing on them if they couldn't shoot back?

"What's going on?" Mel whispered insistently beside him.

"About a hundred of Huayar's men are coming down the hills and shooting at us."

"So shoot back!"

"Can't. We're here strictly on a search-and-rescue. No authorization to engage in a firefight."

She looked appalled. "Do you people need me to run down into the middle of camp so you'll technically be rescuing me?"

"It would help." The comment slipped out before he thought about it. And he knew it was a mistake the second the words left his mouth.

Melina was up and on her feet, darting down the hill before he could make a swipe at her and grab her. Dammit! He jumped up and took off running after her, calling into his mike as he went, "Melina is entering camp from the south end. Bring all resources to bear on her and keep any hostiles from approaching her!"

Hathaway shot back, "What's she doing?"

"Turning this fiasco into a search-and-rescue so we can open fire, dammit!"

A short pause, then Hathaway replied, "You heard the man. All hands are greenlighted to fire to protect the lady."

John's eyes went wide as he realized what Hathaway had in mind. All of his men would fire into the camp—aiming nearly at Melina—and knock out any person who approached her. They would lay down a veritable wall of covering fire around her. It was incredibly dangerous. A single bullet off target would kill her. One unlucky ricochet, one round passing through a hostile and striking her, and she'd die. Hathaway expected her to stand out in the middle of the fish barrel while all of Bravo Squad fired around her.

Sure, it was an exercise they practiced in their hostage rescue training, to shoot around the innocent, missing the victim by a whisker while they took out the hostiles. But that innocent was Melina! And there was nothing to stop Huayar from turning his weapon on her and taking her out except his lust for a drug recipe, and the wealth and power it represented.

Melina screeched to a halt in the dead center of the camp, where the bonfire had been until the flood of water extinguished it. She shouted up into the night, "Here I am! Come and get me, Huayar!"

A dozen hostiles rushed her...and dropped in a neat ring around her.

John's earpiece erupted once more. "...more incoming fire from our flanks...hostiles in sight on the ridge...request instructions..." And then shots rang out behind John. He ducked as a chip of wood flew up from the log above his head. He ducked and took cover from the advancing wave of hostiles from above.

He desperately wanted to join Melina, but these guys would shoot him in the back long before he reached her. He had to take them out first.

Hathaway's disgusted voice came across the radios. "Screw this. Fire at will, men. Take these assholes down. All of them."

John's sigh of relief was heartfelt. Hathaway had probably just thrown away his career, but he'd also given Bravo Squad and the Montez family a fighting chance at getting out of here. It was a ballsy call, but ultimately the right thing to do. God bless Brady Hathaway.

A barrage of lead from above drew his attention. The Peruvians might be good, but he and his gear were better. He flipped on the heat-painting feature of his night-vision goggles, and the hidden forms of Huayar's men leaped out in bright, white relief. He picked them off like ducks in a shooting gallery. It probably took less than a minute to wipe out every form on the hill, but it felt like much longer to him.

Every blob that tumbled down the hillside was therapeutic. How many times he'd played this scenario in his head, of being healthy and armed and able to shoot back at his ambushers, he couldn't count. But dammit, this time he wasn't going down without a fight.

A second wave of hostiles came into sight on the hillside. This bunch had figured out his location, and he was forced to move. He made a shooting retreat down into the camp, using the nearest shack for cover as he made his way toward Melina. *Hang on baby, I'm coming.*

Somewhere in the midst of carnage, an odd thing happened. Peace came over him. An inner quiet he hadn't known for a long time. Death was his job, but it wasn't who he was. He was the man who loved Melina, who Melina loved back. He didn't seek to kill and took no pleasure in it, but he didn't hesitate when it was called for. His adversaries asked for no quarter, as he and his men asked for none in return. Some fights were to the death, and you only lost one of those. For eight of his men, a cold mountain in Afghanistan had been their one and only run of bad luck.

Maybe tonight would be his moment, maybe not. But until that moment came, his job was to keep living. And loving. He glanced over his shoulder and caught sight of Melina. She had her hands over her ears, her eyes screwed tightly shut, and she looked frightened beyond belief.

He yelled into his radio, "Bravo Squad! Hold your fire! I'm going in to join Melina."

"Are you nuts?" Hathaway bit out.

"She can't take it alone. I say again, hold your fire!" he shouted back into his radio as he sprinted toward her, standing there alone and terrified in the center of hell.

Melina couldn't wrap her brain around what was happening. Men were falling all around her like toy soldiers. Falling singly. Falling in waves. Covering the ground in a carpet of blood and bodies thick enough to walk on without ever touching dirt. Bullets flew past her so close she felt them brush her cheeks, her arms, her belly. And Huayar's men kept on coming, and kept on dying.

Why one of them hadn't just raised his gun and shot her before now, she had no idea. Huayar must have given some sort of order not to kill her. Where was he, anyway? She'd seen no sign of him since he ran out of the shack a lifetime ago, when the water tower collapsed.

Hot lead caressed her neck, lifting her hair away from her skin with its passage, and yet another man fell, this time practically at her feet. She would have jumped back from him, but dared not move within the sarcophagus of flying lead hemming her in. Dead eyes stared up at her, impossibly young, as naïve and misguided as her brother. Oh, God. That boy had a mother. A father. Maybe a sweetheart somewhere. And now he was dead. In an instant—

Strong arms swept around her from behind.

"Mel."

She turned in his embrace and jumped as the sound of gunfire, momentarily interrupted, resumed. "You shouldn't be out here! Huayar's men will kill you. They won't shoot me. Get down—"

He kissed her, probably to silence her as he sank straight down to his knees, pulling her down with him. "I love you," he murmured against her mouth.

Joy erupted in the midst of her stark terror. "I love you, too, but I don't want you to die. Get down!"

He glanced at the carnage around them. "Bravo Squad has it about handled. I don't see anymore of Huayar's men incoming. I trust my comrades with my life."

She gazed up at him, startled. "Really?"

He blinked down at her as if just registering what he'd said. "Yeah, I guess so."

"Did you mean it?" she murmured against his neck.

"Mean what?"

"That you love me."

"Absolutely."

"What are you planning to do about it?" she asked cautiously.

"Get you and your family out of here and then at the first opportunity ask your father for permission to marry you."

The gunfire around them was definitely beginning to trail off. A few scattered shots were still being fired well up in the woods, but that was all. *Marry her?* She stared up at him in shock, afraid to believe her own ears. Hesitantly, she asked, "Are you serious?"

"As a heart attack, baby."

She stared up at him in awe, her heart in her throat. John froze, obviously listening to something over his headset, and then laughed.

"What?"

"Your forehead was pressing against my throat mike, and our last several sentences were transmitted to Bravo Squad. My boss just asked what your answer was."

A hot flush climbed her cheeks.

John gazed down at her expectantly. "What should I tell him?"

"Tell him I said yes!" She flung her arms around his neck and all but knocked him to the ground. He staggered, absorbing her weight into him. He absorbed her heart into him, her hopes and fears, her past, her future, all of it. And she let him have all of her. After all, they'd been to hell and back together, and had nothing to hide from one another at this late date.

Concerned that he'd just been through another highly stressful firefight, she asked him with a certain caution, "How are you doing?"

"Fine."

She studied him closely. He looked and sounded like he meant it. "No flashbacks?"

He laughed ruefully. "Oh, there were flashbacks, but I killed most of them. Turns out a little .42-caliber therapy went a long way toward making me feel human again." As she continued to look at him skeptically, he added, "Really. I feel okay. Steady. Centered. I still want to talk to a pro when we get back home, but I think the worst of it has passed. I think maybe we just made it."

She never, ever thought she'd hear those words from him. Had the slate really been wiped clean? For both of them?

He listened to his headset again, then murmured, "Your family has been secured. We found a rat hole and a team of our guys is clearing it right now."

"A rat hole?"

"An escape tunnel. My boss says you and I are to sit tight right here. A team will be over to collect us once they've secured the remainder of the camp and the surrounding hills."

"No more thoughts of nooses?" she asked him.

"None."

"No more wild plans to randomly sacrifice yourself to the bad guys to punish yourself, or in order to save me?"

"Well, I'll always be willing to lay down my life for you. But no, no random sacrifices."

"Thank God." She hugged him tightly, and he hugged her back just as tightly. They'd both faced down Death and managed to walk away from the experience. In finding love for one another, they'd each found a reason to live.

A future she'd hardly dared to allow herself to think about now stretched away before them, clean and fresh and unwritten. And to think. They would get to shape that future together. It was enough to choke a girl up a little.

"You're an amazing man, John Hollister," she whispered against his neck.

"You're pretty amazing yourself, Melina Montez," he murmured, his lips moving against her temple.

She snuggled into his arms and laid her head on his shoulder, content to stay right here for as long as he'd have her. Forever and beyond. After all, they'd already been to hell and back. The only place left for them to go was Paradise. Together.

* * * * *

In honor of our 60th anniversary,
Harlequin® American Romance® is celebrating by featuring an all-American male each month, all year long with
MEN MADE IN AMERICA!
This June, we'll be featuring American men living in the West.

Here's a sneak preview of
THE CHIEF RANGER by Rebecca Winters.

Chief Ranger Vance Rossiter has to confront the sister of a man who died while under Vance's watch…and also confront his attraction to her.

"Chief Ranger Rossiter?" The sight of the woman who'd stepped inside Vance's office brought him to his feet. "I'm Rachel Darrow. Your secretary said I should come right in."

"Please," he said, walking around his desk to shake her hand. At a glance he estimated she was in her midtwenties. Her feminine curves did wonders for the pale blue T-shirt and jeans she was wearing. "Ranger Jarvis informed me there's a young boy with you."

The unfriendly expression in her beautiful green eyes caught him off guard. "Yes," was her clipped reply. "When we arrived in Yosemite the ranger told me I couldn't go anywhere in the park until I talked to you first."

"That's right."

"Knowing you wanted this meeting to be private, he offered to show my nephew around Headquarters."

So this woman was the victim's sister.... "What's his name?"

"Nicky."

The boy who haunted Vance's dreams now had a name. "How old is he?"

"He turned six three weeks ago. Were you the man in charge when my brother and sister-in-law were killed?"

"Yes. To tell you I'm sorry for what happened couldn't begin to convey my feelings."

The woman's gaze didn't flicker. "I won't even try to describe mine. Just tell me one thing. Was their accident preventable?"

"Yes," he answered without hesitation.

"In other words, the people working under you fell asleep on your watch and two lives were snuffed out as a result."

Hearing it put like that, he had to set the record straight. "My staff had nothing to do with it. I, myself, could have prevented the loss of life."

Ms. Darrow's expression hardened. "So you admit culpability."

"Yes. I take full blame."

A look of pain crossed over her features. "You can just stand there and admit it?" Her cry echoed that of his own tortured soul.

"Yes." He sucked in his breath.

"I work for a cruise line. Aboard ship, it's the captain's responsibility to maintain rigid safety regulations. If a disaster like that had happened while he was in charge he would have been relieved of his command and never given another ship again."

Rachel Darrow couldn't know she was preaching to the converted. "If you've come to the park with the intention of bringing a lawsuit against me for negligence, maybe you should." It would only be what he deserved.

"Maybe I will."

In the next instant, she wheeled around and hurried out of his office. Vance could have gone after her, but it would cause a scene, something he was loath to do for a variety of reasons. In the first place, he needed to cool down before he approached her again.

The discovery of the Darrows' frozen bodies had affected every ranger in the park. A little boy had been orphaned—a boy whose aunt was all he had left.

* * * * *

Will Rachel allow Vance to explain—and will she let him into her heart?
Find out in
THE CHIEF RANGER
Available June 2009 from Harlequin® American Romance®.

SUSPENSE

COMING NEXT MONTH

Available May 26, 2009

#1563 KINCAID'S DANGEROUS GAME—Kathleen Creighton
The Taken
Any time things get too difficult, Brenna Fallon runs away. So when private investigator Holt Kincaid shows up, wanting to bring her to her family, she buys time by asking him to find the daughter she once gave up. But when the child is kidnapped, Brenna must enter the highest stakes game of poker she's ever played as Holt searches for the girl, and both soon realize they're gambling with their hearts.

#1564 THE 9-MONTH BODYGUARD—Cindy Dees
Love in 60 Seconds
Tasked with protecting Silver Rothchild as she revives her singing career, Austin Dearing must also guard the baby she's secretly carrying. As attacks on Silver become more intense, she's driven into his arms, and their attraction is undeniable. But can Austin protect Silver enough to keep their romance from crashing to an end?

#1565 KNIGHT IN BLUE JEANS—Evelyn Vaughn
The Blade Keepers
Once he'd been her Prince Charming. But when Smith Donnell took a stand against his powerful secret heritage, he had to give up everything—including beautiful heiress Arden Leigh. When his past came back to threaten Arden, Smith had to emerge from the shadows and win back her trust—and heart—to save them both.

#1566 TALL DARK DEFENDER—Beth Cornelison
Caught in the crossfire of an illegal gambling ring, Annie Compton appreciates the watchful eye of former cop Jonah Devereaux, but she insists on learning to protect herself. As their attraction grows, they dig deeper into the case, danger surrounding them. They'll need to trust each other if they want to defeat these criminals.

SRSCNMBPA0509